THE COOK

'Each time you think you've reached the limit of this thought-provoking and brilliant novel, it just gets deeper.' *Guardian*

'Irresistible—*The Cook* reminds us just how exciting it is
to read a wonderful and original novel.' Lloyd Jones

'The orgiastic pretensiousness of high-end cuisine is a world
that's ripe for satire, and that's just the starting point for this
original, ambitious and disturbing Australian novel...What begins
as a succinct skewering of culinary pompousness...turns into a
scathing commentary into the failings of consumerism...
[a] focused, rapier-like attack.' *Glasgow Herald*

'A writer who is quintessentially of his place and time...*The Cook*,
a darkly satirical reply to Australia's *MasterChef*-driven reality
cooking show obsession, was one of the most surprising and
vivid fictions of the year.' *Australian*

'A compelling read...as tightly structured as a thriller...
hilarious...consistently entertaining, often shocking...a serious
critique of the moral vacuum at the core of a society that
values money and novelty above all else.' *Irish Examiner*

BLUEPRINTS FOR A BARBED-WIRE CANOE

'Wayne Macauley has the soul of a poet and his surreal
novella is stunningly written...It is a satire of exquisite
poise and confidence...If more Australian literature
was of this calibre, we'd be laughing.' *Age*

'Tapping the hidden heart of a different Australia...this is
original Australian writing at its best.' *Courier-Mail*

Wayne Macauley is the author of three highly acclaimed novels: *Blueprints for a Barbed-Wire Canoe*, *Caravan Story* and, most recently, *The Cook*, which was shortlisted for the Western Australian Premier's Book Award, a Victorian Premier's Literary Award and the Melbourne Prize Best Writing Award. He lives in Melbourne.

waynemacauley.com

DEMONS
WAYNE MACAULEY

TEXT PUBLISHING MELBOURNE AUSTRALIA

textpublishing.com.au

The Text Publishing Company
Swann House
22 William Street
Melbourne Victoria 3000
Australia

First published in 2014 by The Text Publishing Company

Cover and page design by W. H. Chong
Typeset by J&M Typesetting

The quotes from *Three Sisters* and *The Cherry Orchard* are from Peter Carson's translations in *Anton Chekhov: Plays* (Penguin, 2002); quotes from Dostoevsky's *Demons* from the translation by Richard Pevear and Larissa Volokhonsky (Vintage, 2006); and the epigraph from a letter written by Kleist to Wilhelmine von Zenge, November 16, 1800. The translation is by Peter Wortsman, from his Afterword to *Selected Prose of Heinrich Von Kleist* (Archipelago, 2010).

Printed in Australia by Griffin Press, an Accredited ISO AS/NZS 14001:2004 Environmental Management System printer

National Library of Australia Cataloguing-in-Publication entry:
Author: Macauley, Wayne
Title: Demons / by Wayne Macauley.
ISBN: 9781922147363 (paperback)
ISBN: 9781922148391 (ebook)
Dewey Number: A823.3

This book is printed on paper certified against the Forest Stewardship Council® Standards. Griffin Press holds FSC chain-of-custody certification SGS-COC-005088. FSC promotes environmentally responsible, socially beneficial and economically viable management of the world's forests.

This project has been assisted by the Commonwealth Government through the Australia Council, its arts funding and advisory body.

Australian Government

Australia Council
for the Arts

MIX
Paper from
responsible sources
FSC® C009448

For my sisters

It holds, I replied, because all the stones want to cave in at once...

Heinrich von Kleist, on observing an arch at Würzburg

FRIDAY

They were going to tell stories. Let's go away for the weekend, said Megan, and leave our phones behind and turn off the computers and the television and stop time because time is moving too fast and soon we'll all be saying where the hell did our lives go? We'll cook some food and drink some wine and each tell a story.

There would be no kids. No pets. No devices. The house belonged to Megan and Leon's younger sister, Lucy—she and her husband, Tom, had moved to Sydney for work. A two-storey perched high on a hill overlooking the sea, just off the Great Ocean Road. A steep driveway, a carport at the top, three bedrooms up and one down. Same road in and out. A cantilevered balcony looking over the trees.

Megan and Evan got down about four, Adam and Lauren just after half past, Leon and Hannah a bit after that. They were living in the bush near Halls Gap now, in the stone cottage Leon built. By five o'clock the smell of slow-braised lamb already filled the house and the wood heater was blazing.

It was the middle of winter, and the forecast was for rain.

Megan was a filmmaker, documentaries mostly. Strong-boned, olive skin, no makeup, short brown hair. She'd been working with the communities up in the Territory, interviewing old people, editing down the footage and sending out group emails about how amazing it was to watch people tell their stories like that. We don't know how to listen any more, she said. Well? What do you say? We'll go down Friday night, come back Sunday. Maybe a couple of days together will be enough to get back to something real.

She was with Evan, a musician; short, lean, fit-looking but lately gone a bit to seed. He used to make his money as a cash-in-hand builder but was now doing up and selling. He was younger than Megan, forty-two, and still had all his hair. They had five kids between them, late teens to early twenties, including a daughter, Aria, from Evan's first marriage.

Adam and Lauren had three kids. Their oldest, Oliver, a problem child, was in his last year of school. Adam was a lawyer, intellectual property, specialising in litigation. He wore his grey hair swept fashionably back, was pale, medium height, with not much fat on him. Clients commented on his pianist's fingers. Lauren was in advocacy and travelled a lot; short, compact, dyed red hair and red lipstick. She went to the gym four nights a week no matter what city she was in. She wore rings and bangles, sensible shoes, had a pointed energy about her and a clipped way of speaking. They'd been together since uni.

Next there was Leon, Megan's younger brother, stocky with a round face that had in its time been ravaged by drink but was now showing good signs of recovery. A journalist, retired. He was bald on top and what was left around the sides was razored to a shadow. There was something a bit distant about Leon. He'd beaten the grog with naturopathy, meditation and yoga and the cure had clung to him almost as persistently as the disease. Hannah, his girlfriend, his *new* girlfriend, was the youngest. She had long legs, Hannah, a long torso and long red hair. She was either wistful or stupid, depending where you stood. She wore a bit of dark around the eyes and a smear of gloss on the lips. They had no kids, together or apart.

The last of that group to agree to put aside that cold weekend in winter were Marshall and his wife, Jackie. Marshall was a politician, newly-elected; Jackie worked in events promotion. But by eight o'clock they still hadn't showed.

Megan and Evan took the main bedroom, with the view of the sea. The other rooms were down the hallway past the bathroom with a view up through the trees. The latecomers got the bedroom downstairs. After everyone had unloaded their stuff and dropped the bags of food and drink in a row on the kitchen floor, Megan suggested a walk. The dark was coming down. She and Lauren, then Leon and Hannah, put on their hats and coats and scarves. Put the meat in the fridge! said Lauren, from the bottom of the stairs.

Evan found the cooler bag with the beer in it and twisted the top off two. Are you into this? he said. Adam put his beer on the bench and started unpacking the meat. I reckon we should have themes, said Evan, like politics or the environment or technology or love or something, otherwise everyone's just going to rabbit on about any old crap. We should write down half-a-dozen and put them in a hat then someone chooses one and we tell stories about that. Then, if we've got the energy, we choose another one later.

They unloaded the shopping and went into the living room. It was warm in there now. At one end was a big set of windows and a sliding glass door that opened onto the balcony that looked out over the treetops to the sea. Two couches, four big armchairs and in the centre a low table of sea-worn timber with a stack of magazines and picture books on it.

Adam stood by the fire. On the wall behind was a painting in pastel tones of sky, sea and dune, the paint dripping from the border of one into the body of the other. Out in the real world, beyond the glass, the ocean was gun-metal grey with a violet sheen and a silver ripple and above it a sunset sky already deepening into dark. Adam slid the door back. The sea was loud, you could feel the *thud* of the waves. Rosellas screeched in the treetops, flew up, wheeled, then hurtled down the hill.

What do I think? said Adam, belatedly. I think the idea of having themes and taking turns is stupid. This weekend we should throw away the rule book, let time stretch out before us. A different kind of time. Story time.

Story time! said Evan.

Yeah, said Adam, closing the door, because that's the kind of time we've lost; everything now is frantic time, desperate time, snatched time. So this weekend we lie on the couch, smoke our pipes, let the pot bubble on the stove.

Evan nodded but he wasn't listening. He was looking back through the living room to the rest of the house.

It's a dog's breakfast this place, isn't it? Ad? He was pointing with the neck of his stubby. The kitchen's all wrong for a start; they should have incorporated it into the living area and orientated it towards the view so while you're cooking you can still talk to your guests and they can see out the windows. You've got more natural light then, too. I'd knock out that wall, he said, and run the bench and cupboards along there, turn that space into a walk-in pantry and take the dining room out through there. And it's stupid having the fourth bedroom downstairs, that should be the recreation area, then you incorporate the downstairs bathroom into it so you can have showers and dump your sandy things when you get back from the beach. Then in the open area there you have your table tennis table and so on. Then up here, you extend the whole joint out that way—he pointed again—at the end of the hall, to create the fourth bedroom. That's just wasted space back there, behind the house, with the washing line and that. Then I'd knock down the carport and turn it into outdoor entertaining, take in the new wet area, reroute the driveway so the cars go round the back and plant it all out, all that area along the fence and up the embankment, with low to medium local natives so it becomes the intermediate space between beach and house and the upstairs part, the big space here, becomes more like a chill-out zone for eating, drinking, reading, watching telly, listening to music. Then I'd pull down that balcony—it looks like the fuckin' prow of the *Titanic*—and put up something quarter-size so you actually take full advantage of the view.

The downstairs door opened and the walking party made their way upstairs. Lauren's got one! said Megan. Suicide, or attempted suicide.

Is that a theme? said Evan.

Megan took off her scarf. Is that your second? she said.

The lamb was brilliant: slow-braised in a big Chasseur with a side serve of Leon's kale. He'd brought broccoli too, and spinach. The wines were top-notch. That's the Heathcote, said Evan: Ad, try that, that's the Heathcote. Everyone except Leon tried the Heathcote.

Evan reckons they should knock down that wall, said Adam, and make all this kitchen and living; move the fourth bedroom up here, knock down the carport, turn downstairs into recreation and open it out onto a landscaped barbecue area with natives.

I can see that, said Lauren. Not in summer though, said Leon; that's a fire hazard, that. They started eating. Because of what Leon said Lauren told a story she'd heard from a friend about a volunteer firefighter who was actually the arsonist who'd started the fire that burned down his town, including his house. The friend was there when the arsonist made his confession. That's called impulse-control disorder, said Adam. Leon told a story he'd heard when he was still a journo about a social worker who was found molesting her young male clients and that set off a discussion about facades and secrets that took them through to the end of the meal. They cleared the dishes. Megan told one about her and Leon's cousin who got mixed up with another cousin, a girl called Philomena, and how it was discovered by—it took Megan forever to explain this—their uncle, but, she said, not the father of Philomena or the cousin but the father of a different cousin again, Megan and Leon's mother's younger sister's husband. Leon said Hannah had a similar story, and she told it.

It was generally agreed, then, after that first round of impromptu stories, that when the real storytelling began they would try not to make them all about family and forbidden sex.

All right, said Lauren, once everyone was seated in the living room. The sky had darkened and a full moon was rising over the water. The sea was loud, but faraway loud. All right, she said, I'm going to start. My story is called *Woman Killed By Falling Man*.

Are we going to give them titles? said Evan.

Adam, said Hannah, do you think we should give them titles?

Titles are good, said Adam.

Wait, said Megan. She handed Lauren the piece of driftwood she'd brought back from the beach. The story stick, she said.

Well, said Lauren, I heard this story from a friend of my sister's. (Adam, don't spoil it.) It was about this friend of hers. Her name was Carly, Carly Ashburton, she worked in cultural programs for local government. My sister's friend worked in council too. An awful story: do you want to hear it?

Everyone nodded.

Well, she said, it seemed Carly Ashburton was going through some sort of marriage crisis. They *should* have been happy, this couple: the children had left and were happy, a son in Europe, a daughter in America. But they'd been married a long time and they weren't happy, that's the truth.

The husband was on sleeping pills and anti-depressants and had actually tried to kill himself. He'd spent the last year in therapy.

Wait, said Evan; the couple, the couple. Has the other half got a name? Tim, said Adam. Tim, said Lauren—he ran a consultancy business in the city, contracts with state government, getting infrastructure into new housing projects. Can I go on?

So, anyway, said Lauren, the husband, Tim, had got it into his head that the main cause of his depression was the quiet of the suburbs (they had a house in Auburn). He wanted to buy a city apartment—he was making bucketloads, after all—and be closer to work. He wanted to live the city life—cafés, bars, restaurants, movies, theatre—and he wanted Carly to live it with him. But Carly wanted different. She wanted to get away from the rat-race, not closer to it. She wanted a treechange.

Well, eventually she wore Tim down; he could see it was going to get messy otherwise. They found a country place out past Sunbury, an old bluestone church on a couple of hectares tucked in off the road in a stand of cypress trees. They picked it up for a song, gutted it, and started rebuilding: a big open-plan living area and kitchen downstairs, mezzanine bedroom upstairs. But does real estate bring happiness? Really?

Everyone looked at Evan. Evan shrugged.

Lauren: Woman Killed By Falling Man...

With her husband working long hours in his office in the city, said Lauren, and she 'between jobs' while they renovated, Carly Ashburton spent her days watching the fine body of the carpenter working. He was Tim's cousin, Jay, and he was doing it cheap. He was not much older than her son.

Oh no! said Hannah. Lauren smiled.

After she'd bedded him once she couldn't stop; it was like a disease. Meanwhile, Tim drove home from work every evening to the sawdust and the offcuts and the water for the pasta bubbling on the two-burner camp stove and kissed Carly's cheek without giving anything away. He was at it every lunchtime with his work colleague, Adele—a marketing manager not much older than his daughter—who lived, ironically, in a high-rise apartment just like the one Tim had dreamed about, with even a view from her bedroom window of their office building across the river.

But of course, said Lauren, it was just a matter of time. Carly was already wondering where her infidelities would take her, her husband where his would take him. He was certainly getting more brazen. He and Adele sometimes even stood out on the balcony in their bathrobes smoking a post-coital cigarette (at home he never smoked), watching the seagulls rise and fall on the updraft from the river, their office just a stone's throw away. It was like they were asking to be seen. As for Carly, she knew her affair with Jay the cousin-carpenter couldn't last (he was already fitting the benches) so with one eye on the clock and one hand on her heart she started to go at him more furiously, in places and positions more outrageous than before, with a kind of reckless, catch-me-if-you-can abandon.

Tim and Adele, meanwhile, had begun to share their after-sex cigarettes in silence. Eventually he had to tell her: he thought his wife knew. Adele's first reaction was to laugh. What difference does it make? she said. What do you care? Tim tried to explain how, in spite of his strong feelings towards her, his very strong feelings, he said, he was still a married man, still had obligations and, he was not afraid to say it, still had feelings for his wife. Adele wasn't happy, naturally. She thought she had Tim to herself and soon let him know about it. He said he understood how she felt, really he did, but, he continued, pleading, surely she could see it from his point of view? He never said he'd leave his wife, on the contrary, he went home to her every evening. But Adele wasn't listening. I suggest you go home, she said, and sort a few things out—if, that is, you have any intention of seeing me again.

Tim left work early that day a changed man (yes, Adele had freed him), determined to go back to his bluestone church and tell his wife how much he loved her, how he'd decided to quit his job and work from home from now on, how they'd plant vegetables and fruit trees, starting tomorrow, how he'd be close to her, always, and their new life could begin. The further he drove, the further away his troubles seemed. He now had almost to squint his mind's eye, so to speak, to bring Adele's face and body into focus or to feel anything for her.

When he pulled into the driveway behind Jay's ute and stepped out of his car that afternoon he felt completely strange and new. The air hummed with an unfamiliar silence. The light was all askew. Even his body felt different, unworn by those few extra hours of work. It was only when he was on the doorstep (the side door, they never went up the wedding steps at the front) that he was overtaken by an even stranger feeling. He shouldn't be here, it was not his time of day; he'd thought only about what he was running away *from*, not what he was running *to*. He listened to the silence; there was no hammering, no sawing, no FM radio playing. Then in that silence he found what he now realised he was listening for: a whimper, a groan, the sound of a chair scraping across the timber floor. He listened a bit longer, then walked back to his car.

Carly heard him: the footsteps on the gravel, the sound of the car door, the ignition, the motor, the whine of the gearbox as it reversed out of the drive. Jay had tied her to the kitchen chair, as she'd asked. From his position he wouldn't hear much—if anything, she thought, as she squeezed her thighs a little tighter. She listened to her husband's footsteps going. What would happen would happen. She leaned back, closed her eyes, and pushed her tongue a little harder against her teeth.

Tim spent the rest of that afternoon in the pub at Diggers Rest. He drank light beer, so as to keep his head, and bought a bottle of white wine before leaving. He arrived home at 'the usual time'. He and his wife drank the wine over a meal of mushroom tortellini and green salad while talking about their renovations. The smell of sawdust was thick in the air. They packed away the dishes and turned the television on. They went to bed early and slept back to back.

So, said Lauren, as you can imagine, Tim went to work the next morning in a pretty foul mood. He had given his wife the chance to come clean. It's not as if I haven't tried, he thought: didn't I agree to the country move, bend my will to hers, give her everything she asked? And this is the thanks I get? All right, he thought; if that's the way you want to play it.

While Carly Ashburton steeled herself the next morning to tell Jay the carpenter that their ridiculous affair was over, her husband, Tim, even before morning tea, had cornered Adele the marketing manager in the photocopy room, apologised for yesterday's mess and begged to come around to her place after work to show her how serious he was.

The end of the day was a long time coming, the path of emotions leading to it jagged and steep. His wife had been having an affair, right under his nose, with his cousin, a tradesman half his age! Tim made some calls, answered some emails; at five he packed his briefcase. He felt like he'd been cut loose; anything could happen. He went to the toilet, washed his hands, and stared at the mirror. He was just stepping into the elevator when his secretary called out. His wife, Carly, was on the line. Did he want to speak to her? Tim paused, thinking, then the elevator doors closed.

What did she want? And what was she to him now? He was free, had been freed. The elevator moved. But perhaps she knew he knew, perhaps she was ringing to confess? Why hadn't he thought of that? He couldn't *hate* her, he'd known her half his life, they'd shared everything together, and yes, the more he thought about it the more he came to see that, despite her infidelities (her *mistakes*, he told himself), he could still love her, even forgive her. With a bit of love and forgiveness they might put all their errors behind. His forthcoming rendezvous with Adele suddenly felt filthy and absurd. But he couldn't turn back; he had to balance that part of the ledger too. He walked across the bridge—a white plastic bag swirled above the water on the breeze—and made his way to her building.

She greeted him in her office clothes. There was a steely resolve coming off her. She wanted to talk. She was not going to delude herself, she said, she knew this was just an affair but, the fact was, she had only been able to go on with it by pushing the thought of his marriage—his wife, his children, his bluestone church—from her mind.

She poured them both a glass of wine. Tim stood at the glass door to the balcony, the city buildings shining gold. He needed a cigarette but he knew it was too early yet. Now Adele was crying. (*My God, what next?*) Couldn't you have kept lying? she said, between sobs. Couldn't you have kept the thing here, in this apartment, between us? He'd still not had a chance to speak, and now he was getting annoyed. He wanted to give her a piece of his mind, but on the other hand he wanted to get her to bed, make love, and by doing so get revenge on his wife—that, after all, was why he was here. But he had no sooner said this to himself, begun to dwell on her faults and blemishes, than Adele became suddenly very attractive to him again. He looked at her leaning there with one hand on the bench, tears rolling down her cheeks, and with just enough cleavage showing for him to imagine his way in there, and realised how utterly ravishing she actually was. He put an arm around her, kissed her neck, but this only made it worse; she pushed him away, he approached again, then without either of them knowing how it happened they were kissing furiously, stumbling into the bedroom and falling onto the bed.

Tim's blood was now at boiling point: he wanted Adele, wanted to possess her and with that drive home the dagger of revenge for Jay's possession of his wife. He was tearing at her clothes; he heard a button pop and hit the wall behind. He knew he was out of control but he was powerless to stop it. Then Adele rolled out from under him, literally rolled off the side of the bed and landed on the floor with a thud. Tim sat up, deranged, confused—one moment she was there, the next not. Her head popped up beside him. With all his experience of women—two wives, three daughters (two from the first marriage), many girlfriends—he still could not fathom that look. It was a mixture of horror and hatred. I rang your wife, she said, earlier this afternoon, and told her what we've been doing. She stood up, rearranged her clothes and looked down at him. I'm going out to eat, she said—and I don't want to find you here when I get back. And with that she was gone.

What happened next probably took little more than a minute but for Tim it must have felt like hours. He heard the door slam, her footsteps in the hall, the elevator bell, the elevator doors, the elevator descending. He got out of bed and went to the living area. He took a cigarette from the packet on the bench and the half-glass of wine he'd left there. He stepped out onto the balcony. The evening was cool. He could see the light on in his office across the river, the cleaner moving around inside. It was a good job, sure, but why did he do it? What was the point? He drank the wine and put the cigarette to his lips. Then he lowered it again. He leaned against the rail. He was a long way up. He butted out the cigarette and put the glass down. He stepped up and closed his eyes. He swayed slightly. Then he jumped.

Right at that moment—*at that very moment*—Carly Ash-burton was facedown on the floor of the church with a blind-fold on, her fingernails scraping the boards while Jay the cousin-carpenter took her from behind. Strewn around the half-built mezzanine was all the evidence of a long afternoon's indulgence: empty wine bottles and half-full glasses, various pieces of underwear, candle stubs on saucers, a stainless-steel phallus, jars of lubricant. Even now, as the daylight began to fade in the high stained-glass windows, with every part of her body hurting, with every muscle spent, she still bucked furi-ously beneath the carpenter's heaving and still kept repeating in her head: *Catch me, I don't care.* She wanted her husband to come home from work and find her spread out like that, all the evidence of her debauchery on show. She had wanted it all afternoon, but her husband didn't come. She was ex-hausted, dry and torn, Jay under her instructions had to scoop great fingerfuls of lubricant from the jar, but Carly had drunk so much wine by now she was beyond feeling.

She'd hardly slept the night before, she was sure she'd been caught, but still Tim wouldn't accuse her. But neither could she bring herself to confess. Their dinner, during which they gave the truth a wide berth and instead ate mushroom tortellini and drank white wine and frittered niceties back and forth, had left her confused. As soon as Tim was out the door that morning she went to the fridge and took out the leftover half-bottle. She listened to the whine as his car reversed out to the road. She knew Jay would be arriving soon. She finished that bottle and opened another. She heard the ute pull up, Jay unloading his gear; she sculled her glass and poured another. It wasn't possible to stop herself—just because her husband suspected something, did this mean she should turn away from the pleasure? If he wanted to stop it he would have. And anyway, she'd seen him eyeing off all those other women—the marketing manager at work, Adele, for one. She was not going to start ticking herself off now. She let Jay get started—he was fitting the skirting boards—before she locked the front and side doors, gave him the signal, drew him to her, and unclipped the bib of his overalls.

They spent the next hour making love in the usual places and in the usual ways, though it was clear throughout that Carly Ashburton's thoughts were elsewhere. Around mid-morning their passion dwindled. Jay put on his overalls and went back to work, Carly sat in the ramshackle adjoining living area with her wineglass and watched him. An hour later Jay said he had to go—he needed some timber to finish off. Carly Ashburton listened to the distinctive sound of his tradesman's ute going through the gears.

A wattlebird was warbling. In the paddocks on the far side of the main road the scream of a chainsaw rose and fell. She filled her glass again: she was already far gone. She could feel her life unravelling, like the sad uncoiling of a spring. All morning she'd felt it, and the drink would not quell it.

She was angry. Did she need the sound of Tim's cousin's ute to remind her that this time yesterday she had heard, clearly, like the ringing of a bell, *his* car on the same gravel drive? He had been here, had heard her moaning, for all she knew with a glass held to the wall; he had heard everything and yet said nothing. What was his game? Was he going to punish her with his silence? Was this the beginning of some great and complicated revenge? Because in the end, she thought, what is more painful: the guilt of knowing you have transgressed or the absence of punishment for your transgression?

These thoughts and more cluttered Carly Ashburton's head while she drank what was left of the bottle. She'd almost reached the point at which something serious might happen, where everything would fall over into chaos. Then the phone rang. It was her husband's work colleague, the marketing manager, Adele. He's dead, she thought, he's killed himself. He's finally done it.

I'm ringing about your husband, said Adele.

He's not here, said Carly Ashburton.

We've been having an affair, said Adele.

There was silence except for the sound of the two women breathing.

I'm sorry, said Adele. The silence got deeper. Adele said: Listen. But Carly Ashburton hung up.

She opened another bottle, poured herself another glass.

Then with an almost athletic shove she got herself up off the couch, staggered a little, and walked into the kitchen. The breakfast dishes were on the bench. She scraped them, gathered them, put them in the dishwasher and turned it on. She wiped the brand-new benches. With her rubber gloves she did the bathroom. She cleaned the toilet, vomited into it, cleaned it again. She scrubbed around the taps with a nailbrush, cleaned her husband's razor. The anger she'd been toying with rose up inside her like an indigestion. She grabbed her stomach, panted, threw the gloves aside. She put on a coat and went outside.

It was raining; she'd not heard it on the roof. She walked, her feet crunching the gravel, down to the main road where the old church sign still stood. She had no idea where she was going. She started walking towards town but then jumped the barbed-wire fence and headed out across the paddock. The sodden ground gave way beneath her. The cows looked up, deadpan. She struggled up an incline until she came to the single tree at the top. It was dry underneath, with a scattering of fallen branches and cow pats. She sat with her back to it, while down below the cows resumed chewing their cud.

She could see the church, tucked into its cypress grove. She saw Jay's ute arrive, him unloading lengths of timber and taking them in by the side door. After a while she thought she heard him banging, though it could have been another sound, coming from the farmhouse on the other side of the hill. She lay with her head on a fallen branch, listening to the sounds drifting up to her, hearing and sometimes feeling the *drip-drip* from the leaves. She opened and closed her fists. She spent an hour like this, maybe more, until she heard Jay's ute start up. She watched it turn out of the drive and head towards town. She went back down the hill.

Once inside she picked up the phone. There was a layer of woodpowder on it. His secretary answered. He's not here, she said, he's just left. Hang on—can I take a message? No, she said. She put the phone down. She drank from the wineglass and steadied herself against the bench. She went to his bedside chest of drawers and got out his bottle of pills. She emptied it into her hand and lined the pills up on the kitchen bench until they formed a row about half a metre long. She popped one into her mouth and washed it down. It would make her feel better, but it would take a little while to work. She took another. She wandered around the half-renovated church, stopping here and there to inspect Jay's handiwork.

She went back to the kitchen, gathered up the pills, took them back out into the living area and lined them up this time on the low coffee table. She put the wine bottle and the glass down beside them. She pointed the remote control at the television and idly watched. She took another pill, drank a little more. She climbed the steps to the mezzanine, walked through the unplastered stud wall, and from her husband's chest of drawers took out his favourite porno. She went back to the living area and put it on. She watched, listened, a blur of flesh and moaning, as she sipped her wine, kissing and sucking the rim of the glass. She turned it off, and returned it to its place in the drawer. She went to the phone and called Jay's mobile.

Where are you? she asked. He was at home, in the garage. Please come, she said; I need you. There was a silence. It's all right, she said, he's not here, he's working late.

At the door she all but tore the clothes from his body. He could see she was far gone, her eyes were rolling, she kept falling onto him. Her kisses were wet and misdirected. But he couldn't deny it, the idea of taking her like this was already making him hard. He knew he'd have to extricate himself from this mess sooner or later but right now it didn't matter.

It was seven o'clock when Jay at last untied her, removed the blindfold and kissed her on the forehead. I have to go, he said. Carly Ashburton lay spread and naked, drifting in and out of a half-sleep. She was still lying like that when the phone rang. It rang off into the answering machine, then a few seconds later it rang again. Carly stirred. The church was dark. She staggered downstairs. The answering machine cut in again; she lifted the phone. Yes? she said. With the receiver still held to her ear she sank to the floor, repulsed at the way her naked body creased itself into folds of fat flesh. There was a pause, then a sombre, official-sounding voice. Hello? Is that Mrs Ashburton? it said.

She knew she shouldn't be driving, but who was she going to ring? She thought for a second of Lidia, Jay's mother, but just as quickly dismissed it. Instead she concentrated on the task of keeping the car to the left-hand side of the broken white line. She got to the city, found the hospital, and walked through the front doors a little after nine.

Two policewomen were standing outside the door to her husband's room. They straightened up and clasped their hands in front of them as she approached. I'm Carly Ashburton, she said. One of them opened the door for her, like a footman. It was a single-bed room, dimly lit. Her husband seemed to be sleeping. There were tubes coming out of him, his lower body was suspended in some kind of traction, with steel wires and counterweights connected to the ceiling above. Carly turned away: she didn't want to be there, didn't know why she'd come. On top of the wine and the pills and the stench of the hospital the sight of her husband made her nauseous.

You can talk to him, said a voice from behind.

Carly? said her husband from the bed. She turned around, a doctor had followed her in; he smiled and gestured to move close. He's very weak, he said.

She felt like she might vomit all over the patient as she moved to the side of the bed and leaned over. His eyes were half-open; the left side of his face, from the temple to the chin, was so swollen that it looked as if it had been attached there by someone, as a joke. His right eye, the one closest to her, widened.

Carly, Tim whispered, I'm sorry. Carly looked at him, this ugly, broken, helpless thing. I tried to kill myself, he said, but here I am, I survived, I don't know how, I don't know why. He tried to smile but he couldn't. I've been having an affair, he said, straining with the effort. Tell me Carly, please, is something going on with you too?

Carly Ashburton held her nerve. She could hear the hum of the medical equipment and feel the presence of the doctor behind her. Yes, she said, something happened, but it was just a kiss; I wanted to go on with it but I couldn't, Tim, I couldn't. Tim held her gaze (and in that moment Carly Ashburton believed her lie as if it were the truth) then he let out a sigh and sank back into the pillows.

He'll be all right, said the doctor, drawing her over to the other side of the room, but it's going to take time. He will need care, and lots of it. His body will heal but—and here the doctor paused—there is a complication. You've seen the police outside; they will speak to you in a moment. They're still trying to work out the exact circumstances but, well, the fact is, according to witnesses, he jumped from a long way up. About twenty floors, we're estimating. Normally this would be enough to kill a person. But the thing is, Mrs Ashburton, there was someone walking below, a woman— and, well, your husband landed on her; she broke his fall. Your husband doesn't know any of this yet, of course, but, well, the fact is, she was killed by the impact, crushed, literally, and your husband is to be charged with manslaughter.

The door opened. A hushed conversation took place between the doctor and one of the policewomen and Carly Ashburton was ushered to a windowless room down the corridor. She answered their questions—no, her husband's fears were unfounded, she'd not been having an affair, and why her husband would want to do this, their guess was as good as hers. Although, she said, he had been on medication and did seem lately to have grown disillusioned with things generally and work especially. Perhaps it had all just got to him? No, she didn't know what he was doing in that building, up there. She gave the police her contact details. They told her that, regrettably, her husband would have to be charged— but, they said, for some time yet he would remain in the care of the medical staff here.

The woman killed, they said, was actually a work colleague, a woman by the name of Adele. Carly's husband had no memory of the incident but he would have to be told eventually. The police had left it in the hands of the doctor as to the best time to do this. Counselling was available to her, Carly, through the hospital, should she feel the need; they suggested she follow this up.

It was after midnight when Carly Ashburton crossed the hospital car park, pointed the remote and unlocked her car. She was tired, sore, hungry; her brain was a mess. She wanted to go home, sleep it off, but as soon as she thought about this, her bed, the image of what she'd left behind—a house strewn with the evidence of her dishonesty, not to say depravity—was too much for her. How could she revisit the shambles of her life? She sat for a long time thinking about all this, staring at the dark concrete wall in front of her. Then she locked the doors, lowered the seat, and slept.

Everyone seemed to hold their breath, wondering had Lauren finished. She half shrugged as if to say: Yes.

And did they get back together? asked Hannah.

They did, said Lauren.

Did he go to prison? asked Leon.

For a while, said Lauren: yes.

But how could they live with themselves? said Hannah.

They should never have sold the house in Auburn, said Evan. That was the start of their troubles: everything would have been fine if they hadn't sold the house. It always comes back to money with you, doesn't it? said Lauren, but with a sort of smile. Evan drank his wine. Megan rolled her eyes.

I just feel really sorry for them, said Hannah; it's awful how things can go wrong sometimes and you have no control over it. You can't blame either of them for what happened, can you, really? It's like they were caught up in something bigger than them both. We don't stop to make decisions any more. It's like the decisions are making us. I don't think that couple—or the marketing manager, or the carpenter—knew what they were doing, really, it was like someone had chucked them in a river that swept them downstream and all they could do was try to avoid the rocks. But it's like that for all of us, isn't it, a lot of the time, don't you think? They weren't making a real estate decision, Evan; I don't think you think that either.

Hannah speaks! said Evan. He was up off the couch, half standing, half sitting, his glass held high above his head. Everyone smiled. Evan lowered himself and looked around for approval. Leon, next to Hannah, pushed a strand of hair behind her ear and kissed her lightly on the cheek.

It's always tragic, said Leon, when a relationship goes bad. I had some messy ones too, you all know that. Megan, so did you. We're all stumbling through this stuff, doing the best we can. It's a sad story, Lauren; it's a very, very sad story.

But it's a funny one too, said Adam. They all looked at him. The way things happen, he said. It's sad, don't get me wrong, but you've got to see the funny side.

No, said Lauren.

Everyone went quiet.

There was the sound of a car outside and a flash of headlights on the window.

Is he with Jackie? said Megan. Evan looked out, and shook his head. If he thinks he can still get something to eat then he can go fuck himself, she said. Marsh! said Evan, waving, but Marshall was already at the door.

When he got to the top of the stairs he stood for a moment; pale, wavering; as if trying to find his balance. Have you got a drink? he said. That's the Heathcote, said Evan. Marshall took a sip.

Jackie's brother Rylan's just killed himself, he said. What? said Megan. Threw himself from a rooftop café, the fuckin' exhibitionist. Asked his girlfriend to hold his drink. Can you believe that? Sorry, sorry. Hello everybody, sorry I'm late. Really. Evan, that's good. Jackie couldn't come. Go, go, she said; you go. I shouldn't have come, I know—don't look at me like that, please—but she *told* me to, she didn't want me around. I won't go into it, for God's sake, please, don't make me go into it. But maybe I will. This is good. How have you guys been? Have you eaten? I've got to tell you, before we start: things are not good between me and Jackie. I don't know if you know that. She didn't tell me to go, that was a lie. I just did. There's no way I could be around that family while they cried their eyes out over that selfish little prick. Sorry. And you know *why* he did it? Why? Because he'd asked Mummy and Daddy for some money to start up a business—he wanted to do craft jewellery—but they said he had to match them dollar for dollar. So he went to his sister and asked her but she said the same: dollar for dollar or nothing, Rylan, even though she'd usually hand over fistfuls, but she didn't want to disagree with me this time because, well. It's been going on for months. A lazy little slug. Or was. Sorry. How are we all? Have you eaten?

Marshall had recently won a seat in state parliament, last week he was on the news, but he looked like any ordinary person now. Clean-shaven, a boyish face, a few old-man lines, his hair just starting to turn.

You shouldn't have come, mate, said Leon. I know, I know, said Marshall; did you already start the stories? We did one, said Hannah. Maybe we should leave it, said Lauren. No, no, don't worry about me, said Marshall; I'll have a couple of drinks and I'll be fine. I've already told mine, anyway, he said, smiling, about Rylan, the little toad. But we're doing more than one though, yeah?

Megan turned the dimmer up. There was an uncomfortable feeling in the room.

I've got one, said Hannah. No-one was sure what to say. I might get that other bottle, said Evan. That's weird, said Lauren. They all looked at her. My story had a jumper too. Don't worry, said Adam, people are doing it all the time. Evan came back with the wine. Lauren wants us to score her story out of ten, said Adam. What? said Lauren. Hannah? said Evan. Before you start? Hannah held out her glass.

Marsh, are you okay? asked Adam. That's the other Heathcote, said Evan. Tilly's in the car, said Marshall. What? said Megan, standing up.

I had to bring her, he said. I told her it was just adults, she didn't want to come inside. Everyone was staring at him.

No, she'll be right, he said, she's got her phone, let's leave her there, I'll tell her to come in later, she can sleep in my room. All good, all good.

The story stick was on the table, still damp and smelling of the sea. Hannah picked it up.

Well, she said, my story is called *Pan*. Pan? said Marshall. Like dust pan? said Evan. Pan like the Greek god Pan, said Hannah, protector of sheep and goats. He was associated with wild places: forests, mountains. Pan means 'all', said Adam. That's true, said Hannah, and even though Pan was a playful god he could sometimes suddenly turn and the vibe would change and everyone would get frightened and that's where we get the word 'panic'. But anyway, to the story.

This is good, said Marshall.

Lauren's story made me think of it, said Hannah, how Carly wanted to get away, how we all want to get away somehow, somewhere. There's always some dissatisfaction in us, isn't there?

Speak for yourself, said Evan. (Everyone laughed.)

It's about a girl I knew when I was younger, said Hannah, she wasn't really my friend, just one of those girls who hung around on the edges of the group, hard to get to know. We were in our last year of school. Then one day she disappeared. I say one day because that's what it felt like but actually what was happening was she was hanging around with us less and less then hardly at all and it was weeks since we'd seen her when one day we turned around, so to speak, and said: Where's Elena? Her name was Elena. Anyway, I'll tell you what happened.

Hannah: Pan...

Elena lived in a house not far from me with her mother and younger brother, Ty. Her parents had split up. It was an average-looking house, nice, suburban. None of us had ever been inside but my brother, Cody, he knew a kid who was a friend of Ty's and this kid said the house was spotless—you had to take your shoes off at the door. There was every kind of electronic gadget and appliance in there imaginable. The father wasn't rich, but he'd felt guilty about leaving the kids behind. Every night in those last weeks before the break-up he'd come home from work with something new: Ty got a TV, a computer, a PlayStation; Elena herself always had new clothes and things. Her hair was shiny, she seemed to have an endless supply of makeup. In fact, she was the complete opposite of what you would expect an outsider-type like her to be: pretty, sometimes really confident, although most of the time, when I think about it, quiet. When she first got sick and spent time away from school none of us took much notice. Someone one day said: Where's Elena? Someone said she was away and that was it. She's not well, the teachers said. But then she started staying away longer.

The end of the year came—formal, muck-up day, exams—and we sort of forgot about her; we assumed she'd dropped out, and we had bigger things to care about. It wasn't till years later, when I was in my mid-twenties, that I heard what had happened.

Elena had got sick, then sicker. No-one really knew what was wrong with her. Her mother was working full-time and since the father disappeared she'd taken on overtime too, so Elena and her brother were pretty much left to themselves—which was why, at first, Elena did nothing about her illness but stay in bed and take Panadol. But eventually the message came back from the school that if she were to be given special consideration at exam time she would need to get a doctor's certificate.

Ty took the morning off and went with her on the bus. The doctor examined Elena top to bottom but couldn't figure out what was wrong. He presumed it was viral, possibly even glandular fever, and sent her off for some tests. The tests came back inconclusive and she was sent off for more. Her brother accompanied her when he could—his teachers were losing patience too—to those funny medical places in converted suburban houses which might be your auntie's place if it wasn't for the sign in the front yard, the high counter with the brochures on it and the water cooler in the corner. They'd sit on the bus, Elena with her X-rays or CAT scans in a big white envelope, Ty with his Game Boy. Music was Elena's other companion; she took out her earphones for only as long as it took the specialist to say, for example, Please lift up your top, or, Get up on the bed, or, Here's your referral.

After a while Ty stopped coming and Elena did all this on her own. In between the bus trips and consultations she lay on her bed and listened to music or played on her computer. But closing in on all sides always was this awful lethargy, a queasy feeling in her stomach and a low buzz like from a faulty appliance somewhere up in her temples. She was sick, and it seemed as if nothing would make her better.

It was a friend of the family's, a woman called Anna, who suggested one day that maybe Elena should see an allergist. Her son, said Anna, had found out he was allergic to varnish. Elena's mother was so struck by her friend Anna's advice that she took a morning off work. The allergist was a couple of suburbs away in a house with a neat front yard. Elena's mother saw her in, spoke to the receptionist, then left. Elena would make her own way home.

She had only just picked up a lifestyle magazine and started flicking through it when out of the corner of her eye she saw the receptionist leaning over the high front counter, pointing at the door to her right. The allergist was waiting. Elena put the magazine down, took out her earphones, smiled at the receptionist and went in.

The allergist was a middle-aged man named Dr O'Breen, bald on top but with grey-blond hair falling down around the back and sides. His suit needed cleaning, there was a fake flower in his lapel. Hello Elena, come in, he said, nice to meet you. That was funny him saying that, she thought, like their meeting was somehow a surprise and not just another pre-arranged consultation like the dozen she'd already had. He gestured to the chair. On the desk was a black cardboard box with a band of packing tape reinforcing it all the way around the top. The box had begun to split from overuse. It was the kind of packing tape her mother used to patch the old atlas she kept on the top shelf in her bedroom cupboard. A thick rubber band held the lid of the box in place.

Well, said the allergist, I hear you've not been well—do you want to tell me about it? Elena mechanically went through the story, starting from when she had first felt ill at school, including the doctors and specialists she'd seen. O'Breen made a few notes. And you just don't feel well, he said. Is there anywhere in particular? Headaches? An upset stomach? Any rashes or itches? Elena sketched a general picture of how she felt, which in a sense was a combination of all of the above and more, bound together by a constant tiredness that even now made her wish she was out in the waiting room again, her music on, her face hidden in the magazine, her eyes drooping and her mind drifting away into sleep. I see, said the allergist. Well. He moved the black cardboard box in front of him and began to take off the rubber band, something he had obviously done so many times that Elena couldn't help being

34

mesmerised. O'Breen stretched it in and out between his finger and thumb then let it snap onto his wrist. He lifted the lid off the box.

Inside was a wooden tray holding, at a quick glance, about fifty little vials. All these vials had labels; from where Elena was sitting she could see Wool, Latex, Paint, Rayon. Now Elena, said the allergist, we are going to do a few little tests to see if there is something in your daily life that might be making you unwell: to do this I will need you to roll up your sleeve. O'Breen was gesturing with a flat hand at the left sleeve of Elena's cotton top; again it felt like a gesture re-hearsed and performed a thousand times. As soon as the sleeve was up he came around beside her and, scribbling with a black biro on her forearm, explained the procedure. In each spot, he said, I'm going to put a little drop.

There were about a dozen biro marks on Elena's forearm now: strange symbols, numbers, letters, each designating the thing to go there. One by one O'Breen took from the wooden tray a vial corresponding to the marks and put down a tiny drop. Elena read some of the labels as the allergist moved quickly through them: Dog, Cat, Mouse, Dust, Pollen. He deposited the last drop and took a sterilised needle saying, quickly, like it barely needed mentioning: You will feel a little scratch. Then he ran the needle through each drop, scratching the skin as he went. When he'd finished he put the needle into a yellow tub, arranged the vials back in their tray with the labels up, put the lid on the box, slid the rubber band off his wrist, stretched it around and let it go with a snap. O'Breen pushed the box aside. All right, he said, leave your sleeve up, pop out into the waiting room, and after fifteen minutes we'll see what we've got. I'll call you back when we're ready. The allergist had already turned his back on Elena as he went around the desk to his chair. Elena took this as her cue.

Out in the waiting room the receptionist smiled like she must have done a thousand times to a thousand other patients who now had to wait the obligatory fifteen minutes with their sleeves up. Elena smiled in return and sat in a chair next to the disused fireplace.

At one end of the mantelpiece was a small plastic stand displaying brochures about allergy and at the other end, incongruously, a child's rattle. Two chairs down from Elena was a low table with magazines; she picked one up and sat down again. Against the wall beside the receptionist's high counter—sitting down you could only see the top of her head—was a tank with tropical fish swimming lazily around inside, the water bubbling softly through the filter. On a chair against the other wall was the only other person in the room, an old man with his sleeve up like her. He smiled when she glanced at him, and looked down at the arm he was cradling like it was broken, as if to say: You have one too. Elena gave him a brief smile, then to avoid having any more to do with him, she started flicking through her magazine.

The fifteen minutes seemed to go on forever. There was a clock above the receptionist's head and for the first five minutes Elena kept glancing at it, then down at her forearm, trying to make in her own way some connection between the sweeping second hand and the *click-click* of the minute hand and the slower, more subtle, changes going on under her skin. But it soon became a pointless game: the seconds swept by and the scratches on her arm above the black writing describing all those things in nature that might make your life a misery registered no change at all. She flicked again through the magazine until she found something to look at, creased the spine and gave all her attention to the pictures.

It was a design magazine, and the article was about houses built in exotic locations: in a rainforest with a living area built into the canopy, on the side of a hill overlooking the sea with a roof covered by sand and dune grass, and, finally, a house blended into the rock of Sydney Harbour to the extent of actually having a boulder in the living room and a deck built into a craggy outcrop over the water. The owners, said the article, loved food and wine, and the dining-room table at which they entertained was long and curved 'like the beach below', set with baskets of fruit and mini pumpkins and gourds. A sculpture hung above it, a crayfish basket holding seafood carved out of driftwood. Elena was so absorbed with the pictures of this house and the people who must have lived in it that for a moment she didn't notice the receptionist calling her or, for that matter, O'Breen himself, waiting at the door to his room. The doctor is ready, said the receptionist. You can come in now, said O'Breen.

Back in the consulting room Elena sat down while O'Breen brought his chair from around the other side of his desk, settled himself next to her and took her arm in his hands. He had red, flaky patches on his scalp. He was looking at the scratches, first from a distance then up close with a magnifying thing that he put over his eye. It took him a long time to say: No. Elena wasn't sure what he meant. She kept looking at his bald patch while he looked at her arm. No, he said, again, lifting his head and taking off the magnifying thing, nothing there at all. You are at one with Nature, Elena, he said, in a funny, pompous voice, and he pushed himself away.

The little drops I put on your arm, Elena, contained distilled quantities of the substance you see on the label. For example, Mouse. I get them from Spokane, Washington. No-one else does them here. If you were allergic to, say, Mouse, said O'Breen, your skin would come up in a little welt, like a mosquito bite, where I scratched it. The marks in black pen tell me what I have put where and in this case all of them describe common allergens, things we find in the natural world: animals, plants and so on. You'd be surprised how many people are allergic to Mother Nature. He did that smile again. But not you, as you see. So. O'Breen pushed off with his chair and sort of pedalled his way back around behind his desk and in one smooth movement pulled the box in front of him, slid the rubber band from it onto his wrist and took off the lid. Let me see your other arm, he said.

On Elena's left forearm this time O'Breen scratched a drop each of Formaldehyde, Isocyanate, Sulphur Dioxide and Epoxy Resin and sent her out into the waiting room again. This time while waiting she started to think about what O'Breen had said, how he seemed to be making a distinction for her between a natural and an artificial thing and how, yes, especially over the last couple of years, she had become impatient with the artificial in a general sense, be it the cheap Asian-made but fashionable clothes her schoolmates wore or the stupid, superficial things they said. Elena had just started to go a little further with this thought when she realised that fifteen minutes had passed and O'Breen was calling her back.

The diagnosis this time was also straightforward. On each scratch on her other arm the welts were up, an angry red already spreading out beyond the wound itself. O'Breen examined each of these marks, pushing back the skin on either side with his thumbs and leaning down with his magnifying thing. He said nothing, a specialist utterly absorbed in his work; it was only as he drew back and pulled a plastic bottle of cortisone cream across the desk towards him, flicking the cap and offering it to Elena, that he finally said: Yes.

Elena was allergic to everything we might call 'modern'. O'Breen explained how there are, on the one hand, substances we find naturally, in nature, and, on the other, manufactured or artificial substances that we have created molecularly from the ground up. It was the second category, exclusively, that Elena was allergic to and sadly these substances were everywhere.

After that first assessment Elena regularly went back during the following weeks to the house behind the low brick fence with the sign in the yard to be tested for yet another suite of substances. She was allergic to them all. One day O'Breen stood her in her underwear in the centre of the room and ran a wand emitting electromagnetic waves over her body: this too brought her out in a rash and left her with a headache and a queasy feeling that lasted for days. O'Breen prescribed various drugs and creams and started to make up with her what he called an 'action plan', so that she might eliminate these allergens from her life. After the fourth visit the receptionist gave Elena an envelope to take home and on the bus she carefully prised it open. Addressed to her mother, it was the bill so far. Elena hid it in her underwear drawer and never mentioned it again.

She became increasingly withdrawn and strange. She stopped going to school, or went for a few hours only when it suited her. The principal contacted her mother who said Elena was sick, then as she always did her mother went straight to her room and yelled at her to get better.

Elena lived in her bedroom, a spartan space now bereft of

the usual teenage clutter. She took her tablets and rubbed the creams into her skin and bought her own organic food which she ate in there, mostly raw. Without any modern gadgetry to rely on she quickly lost contact with the few friends she'd had—including me, said Hannah.

Then one day, after the usual visit to O'Breen, outside the shopping centre where she habitually changed buses, she let her usual bus go, waited at the stop for a while, and caught the bus to the city instead. She got off at the depot near the station, bought a ticket and boarded another bus that would drop her seven hours later in the tiny coastal town where her uncle owned a small timber cottage where, when they were young, she and Ty would spend the holidays, collecting shells on the beach and fishing in their uncle's boat at dawn on the vast, mirror-smooth lake. She knew where the key was, under the rock, and let herself in.

The cottage smelled shut up and musty—her uncle had been sick in hospital lately and had let the property go—but Elena soon threw open the windows and doors to let the sea breeze in. She spent that first evening eating the woody carrots she'd pulled out of the garden (they must have self-seeded, as had an ad hoc mix of potatoes, pumpkins and spinach), sitting on a kitchen chair outside the front door looking at the pelicans skimming the lake and listening to the surf on the other side of the bar. The sunset was beautiful. She slept that night a peaceful sleep and woke for the first time in months without a headache.

The cottage sat on a small hill above the lake that fed through a narrow channel into the sea. The upper reaches of the lake branched out into rivers and creeks, poking their way up, narrower and narrower, into the high mountains behind. (She and her brother had gone with her uncle one day up one of these rivers, paddling and then dragging their canoes until, high up, they reached the source.) There was a grassy slope below the house with a few tea-tree bushes on it and a clump of denser tea-tree where the land met the water. The nearest house was half a kilometre away. At night you could hear the seagulls squawking and the possums scratching in the roof, and beneath all that, like a low drone, the sea. Aside from the occasional sound of a car gearing down to get up the hill on the far side of the point, there was nothing human out there.

The house was built in the eighties from scavenged timber and tin, and the furniture and fittings all dated from that time. The next morning, after curling up on the couch in a sleeping- bag she found rolled up in the top cupboard, Elena set to work cleaning the house and getting rid of anything she might be allergic to: the clock radio beside the double bed, the portable radio on top of the fridge, the microwave oven, the television, all the old soaps and shampoos and other toiletries from the bathroom; the synthetic curtains, cushions and bed linen. She put all this stuff out in the shed where her uncle kept his boat, the junk he had collected and the timbers and windows left over from when the house was built. She left the fridge in the kitchen—it was too heavy to move—but she didn't turn it on. Last of all she gave the house a clean from top to bottom, but with warm water only, heated on the old wood stove, using a cotton singlet. There was a packet of beeswax candles in the bottom drawer in the kitchen and one by one she set these candles around the house.

That afternoon she went into the garden, wearing the old straw hat she found in the shed, and started pulling out weeds. It felt good out there. It was one thing, she thought, to be told you can't tolerate anything new and artificial and that you must be among only natural things, but it was another to live it. She felt an energy, a vigour, she'd not felt in ages. Even her mood had changed; she was no longer grumpy, pissed off with everyone, disillusioned about who she was; she just *was*, here, now, out in the garden, under the sun, pulling weeds on this bright day. And always, above, behind, beyond all this was the soothing sound of the sea, so unlike the things in the box with the rubber band around it (*Without me how will you wash your hair? Without me how will you drive your car? Without me how will you be entertained?*) that to think of it swelled her soul to twice its normal size.

She spent a good while out in the garden, she seemed to have slipped through a hole in time and come out at a place where clocks didn't count; the day stretched out in front of her; she felt vibrant, alive. When she was tired she'd sit down on the step; when she felt like digging, she'd dig. The soil was sandy loam and the spade cut it easily; before she knew it she had, as well as weeding the five beds already there, dug out the grass and mounded up another five, moulding the furrows between them.

At around four o'clock that afternoon she stopped, stood back to admire her handiwork, then washed herself at the garden tap. She took off her top and bra, unafraid, splashed water under her arms and breasts, turned the tap up full and let the water hammer at the nape of her neck. She dried off, pulled on one of her uncle's old collared shirts from the cupboard—pure cotton, lemon yellow, green buttons and green stitching on the cuffs—and set off around the point into town.

Can I ask you something? said Lauren, quietly. Sure, said Hannah. How old is she now? She's just turned eighteen, said Hannah. Everyone waited. Hannah went on.

The town was small, she said, a main street with a parking island, a pub, a shopfront supermarket, a little restaurant-café, a real estate agent, a takeaway, a gift shop, a tackle shop, and that was about it. It was after five o'clock now, and the town was actually pretty lively, with the sound of voices and horse-racing coming out of the open door of the pub and people walking in and out of the supermarket. A few others were sitting at the tables outside the café; a tanned man in a suit outside the real estate office gave Elena a smile as she passed.

She had enough money to stock up on basic supplies, after that ran out she wasn't sure what she'd do. Already, as she approached the supermarket, she could smell the exhaust fumes and that vague smell—what was it?—of towns and cities: concrete, asphalt, steel, plastic. It sat right up the back behind her temples and she could already feel the headache coming on. She turned into the supermarket, intent on getting what she needed as quickly as she could. She bought bread, milk, butter, unbleached toilet paper, a cigarette lighter (she couldn't use matches because of the sulphur), more candles, vegetables from the little organic section in the fridge at the back and a dozen organic eggs. At the counter a young man served her, he must have been about her age, and Elena couldn't help being conscious of her wet, uncombed hair, her uncle's shirt and the red rash she could already feel coming up around her neck. As he packed Elena's things into the box he kept his eyes down but when he looked up to give it to her she could see he was blushing. Maybe he had allergies too? Thanks, come again, he said, stupidly. Elena nodded and smiled.

The box was heavy and it was a long way back to the house but with the sun setting over the lake and the sky full of seabirds squawking and the air so clean and clear that you could actually *feel* it pushing the bad air out, Elena didn't feel the weight; or rather, felt it as a good thing, and the walk home through that alive and raucous twilight as the start of something good. Back at the house she prepared to settle in; she lit the beeswax candles, then the stove, and cooked herself an omelette with some vegetables cut into it. She couldn't sleep on the bed with its nylon mattress so she took a candle out to the shed and found the rope hammock she and her brother used to lie in under the tree and strung it across the lounge room, anchored at either end by tying a knot and closing the window on it. She put the cotton and duck-down sleeping-bag on it for a mattress, and a cotton sheet and woollen blanket from the linen cupboard over that. She blew out the candles about nine.

In that small house in that faraway town Elena settled into a new routine that took its cue from nature. She woke early, ate a bowl of yoghurt or oats with warm milk, sitting on a kitchen chair in the sun, then she tidied the house and dug the garden. At around three each afternoon she would take a nap in the hammock in the lounge room, letting herself drift through mostly innocuous dreams until a bit after four when she would start thinking about dinner. The meal was always simple, made from the stuff she picked from the garden or had bought at the supermarket. While the evenings were still warm and the days long she ate outside at the little fold-up table on the veranda that looked down the grassy slope towards the lake. She always brought a couple of candles out there, stuck into her uncle's old empty beer bottles, and would often stay until the sky darkened and the birds went crazy and the clumps of tea-tree and the grassy slope and the mountain range beyond turned ink black and all that was left was the glow from the lake. Then she would sit out there by candlelight, looking and listening for mosquitoes, slapping her skin and holding her hand up to see what she'd got (she couldn't use repellent and had thrown the can out when she cleaned the shed), doing little else except occasionally looking out across the lake where on the nights when there were no clouds and a decent moon a silver sheen spread like sheet metal, broken only by the occasional fish breaching the surface or a bird paddling past or by a ripple from the breeze.

She wasn't happy, that would be a strange thing to say, but she'd found a way to be content. She didn't know how long this contentment would last, though compared to her moodiness, anger and confusion back in the city this might be as close to happiness as she'd get. She knew they'd come looking for her eventually, all those people who wouldn't have missed her before, who wouldn't have even known she existed. But she was a whole day's travel away, had got almost to the border; if she kept her head down she'd be okay for a while. Maybe, she thought, she could take some of this good health back to the city with her? Maybe tell others what she'd found? You can't preach for one life over another but you could always show by example.

So that was it, those were her days. Most mornings early she would take the old rod and reel from the shed and the bucket of sandworms she'd pumped at low tide and fish off the jetty below the house until she caught something for dinner. (At first the reel didn't work; she took it apart, piece by piece, then cleaned and lubricated it with oil.) There were mussels, too, out on the rocks, and crabs in the estuary shallows. On moonless nights the prawns would run from the lake to the sea on the tide and all you had to do was stand near the entrance, look out for their frightened phosphorescent eyes and scoop them up in your net.

One morning when she was sitting outside drinking tea at the table a figure appeared at the bottom of the grassy slope where the track wound its way around the lake. She'd some-times see fishermen walking that way, their rods glinting in the early light, but this figure didn't have a rod and had now started to walk up the slope towards her. He pushed his way through the tea-tree and stopped at the fence.

Hello there! he said. Beautiful morning! I'm Lyall from around the corner. It was awkward. Elena sort of half smiled and waved. There was an excruciating pause before Lyall returned the wave and said: Well, have a nice day! Then he headed off back around the track.

The next morning at the same time he was there again, waving, calling out, and this time crawling through the wire and walking a few metres up the slope. You're new, aren't you? he said. Did you buy Peter's place off him? Elena told him Peter was her uncle, he wasn't well; then she left a long pause so Lyall might get the hint to go. Instead he walked a few more metres up. If you ever need a hand with anything, he said, just give us a yell, I'm only around the corner. For the first time Elena got a good look at him: a small-town bogan, early thirties, maybe older, with wiry hair cut into a mullet and a salt and pepper goatee beard. Even from that distance Elena could see the missing teeth.

One day Lyall didn't come from the track but appeared suddenly from around the corner of the house. Elena was just finishing her breakfast, staring at the lake which on that morning held a soft green sheen. Lyall's hair was wet and his goatee trimmed and he smelled of shampoo and aftershave. Good morning, he said, bouncing on his heels. You keep saying you'll let me do things around the house for you but you never invite me up, so I've invited myself up anyway. After that there was a heavy silence. Look, I'm just being a good neighbour, said Lyall, glancing around for a chair to sit on; it's a small town and pretty well everyone knows everyone so it's best we know each other too. I'm Elena, said Elena, and she stood up to shake his hand. It was hard and callused, like an old man's hand. I'll get you a chair, she said. She went inside and came back out with a chair and set it down beside the table for him. Lyall sat on the very edge with his knees splayed and his hands gripping his thighs. So what's your story? he said. Everyone here's got a story. You don't end up miles from anywhere like this unless you're running away from something. Me, it was a bad marriage and then just badness generally. What about you?

Elena told him. She told him about the situation at home then how she fell sick and dropped out of school and didn't know what was wrong with her. She told him about O'Breen and described what went on in his room in great detail. She listed her allergies and the symptoms of each. I'm allergic to the modern world, she said; not enough to kill me but enough to stop me and the modern world getting on. Even your aftershave, now, she said, and your shampoo; they're making me feel not quite right. So I jumped on a bus and came here. Maybe it's temporary, I don't know, I haven't decided yet.

I can go away, said Lyall, if the chemicals are bad; actually, you know, I don't usually wear this stuff, unless I've got something special to go to which I don't very much. Serves me right! Elena smiled. Maybe just go back a little way, she said, on that side over there, so the breeze will take it away.

Elena and Lyall kept talking, once Lyall had moved his chair. Elena's mention of her allergies seemed to open up something in him. Like her, he was there to get away. The city's no good, goodness has fled the city, said Lyall. When was the

last time you met a good person there or saw an act of goodness or had some goodness done to you? Lyall explained how
he had tried to make the city work for him but how the city
was always conspiring against him and how it was not until
he'd left and come here that he realised that he was actually in
a perpetual struggle with the city, like Jacob with his Angel, he
said, and that in fact every day lived in the city was a struggle
with the city; there was always a part of you, even a subcon-
scious part, fighting with it. He explained at great length how
since coming in from the plains and dwelling in houses and
suburbs the human species had always been engaged in this
knock-down-all-in fight with the city which, Lyall insisted,
it will never win. The odds are always stacked in Babylon's
favour, he said. We cling to civilisation's veneer, the idea that
once upon a time in a city somewhere someone painted a
picture or built a beautiful building or made a beautiful piece
of music and that therefore we city dwellers are closer to God,
the Almighty. But no. We make paintings and palaces and
symphonies but we also make shampoo and aftershave and
petrol and plastic and pesticides and computers and computer
games and pornography and chat rooms.

Elena loved listening to Lyall's voice, the rise and fall of
it, the plaintive rhythm, like an old train chugging off into
the mist. It was not so much the words she was hearing as the
soothing sound they made in the air. She let him go on; to
her it seemed somehow that his voice was tuned to perfectly

match their surroundings, that it was a voice that could as easily have been spoken by the trees, the grass, the birds, the lake or the waves on the other side of the bar, and it was surely the voice she had looked for and not found until now. Every other voice she'd heard was shallow, tinny, screeching; the voices of her friends, the voices on the radio, the television, the voices coming out of speakers in shopping centres and railway stations. All that cacophony had faded and here, right up close and at the same time somehow everywhere, was a voice spoken only for her.

The Lord's people were desert dwellers, said Lyall, and the Lord gave unto Abraham all the land he could see to the north and south and east and west so He could make with Abraham a covenant that far from the cities of the Nile and the Euphrates these were his lands, the lands of the plain, and they were like unto the dust of the earth and if you could count the dust of the earth you could count their number and they were many. And the Lord with His mighty hand smote the cities of Sodom and Gomorrah, said Lyall, and rained down fire and sulphur on them because the cities bred wickedness while Abraham's people walked with God, they were pure and like unto the white lambs with their shepherd. And no city was spared God's mighty wrath because in every city the wickedness of man was manifest. And He saw how it was not those iniquitous people of the city that were His chosen but those camped in tents under the stars, tending their flocks and moving across the plains, building stone altars and kneeling in the dust and bowing down to the Lord in honour and thanks; these were His people and these would be blessed and the others would be cursed. And when the Lord God's only begotten Son came down from Heaven didn't He too walk in the dust of Abraham and let the dust of Abraham's people gather in the hem of His garments and didn't He chase the moneylenders from the Temple and say: Woe unto thee Chorazin and Woe unto thee Bethsaida and Tyre and Sidon and thou Capernaum which shall be brought down to Hell? Yea verily we must turn our backs on the cities of the plain and not look behind lest we turn to salt. We must look up and find God, under the stars, in the trees, the grasses, the crystal water of the lake. Behold the birds of Heaven, they sow not, neither do they reap, nor gather into barns; consider the lilies of the field, how they grow, they toil not, neither do they spin.

So I turned away, said Lyall, from the people of the city, and I did not look back while behind me, lo, the smoke went up as the smoke of the furnace and I came here, Elena, to start anew, to be with nature and through her closer to my God. And I didn't look back then and don't look back now—my wife, my children, they are dead to me, consumed in God's mighty fire—and nor should you look back, now that you are here. Those allergies you talk of are the Devil's work and the marks on your skin his stigmata, the Devil's brands. Let Satan be cast behind—Get thee behind me, saith the Lord—so we might raise our eyes to God and see everywhere His good works.

Lyall visited every morning and every morning he spoke like this. They shared cups of tea on the chairs out in the sun and sometimes strolled down the grassy slope and stood looking at the lake. Soon it seemed right that Elena should visit Lyall, and she did. He drew a map of the path from her house to his and one morning carrying the oatmeal biscuits she'd baked she followed it around the lake until she came to the tree with the white mark on it that pointed the way up through the bush.

Lyall's house was not so much a house as a shack, built in among the trees from rough-sawn planks, second-hand timbers, odd weatherboards and sheets of ply and scavenged windows and doors under a corrugated roof. There was a sort of sitting area outside with an old wooden table and a couple of chairs. Above Lyall's door a wooden cross was fixed, and painted on the door itself in one continuous white line— head, body, tail—was a fish. There was a small dog tied to a stake nearby, a scrawny, mangy thing; it didn't bark at Elena's approach but just whined and squeezed its tail a little harder between its legs.

Lyall heard Elena coming and stood at the door to greet her. Welcome! he said. Elena wore her uncle's clothes on the days her own clothes were drying and on this day she had on a pair of creased brown trousers rolled up at the cuffs and pulled in at the waist, and a light blue shirt with vertical white stripes. The day before she'd cut her hair short with blunt scissors. Sit down! Sit down! said Lyall.

It was peaceful out there in the bush, you could hardly hear the waves but there were plenty of other sounds: insects, birds, the scuffling and rustling of animals in the undergrowth, the breeze moving the treetops, the branches creaking. Pretty soon Lyall was talking again about the train wreck of civilisation and the lemmings running over the cliff and all the other things he had on his mind and that sound too soon blended with the others until they became one. Elena's visits grew more regular. One day at the table outside his shack while talking about the pestilence Lyall asked to see Elena's stigmata and in doing so touched her arm. Elena left it there, then withdrew. A bird calling out from a tree somewhere up on the hill was the only thing to break the silence.

Elena grew worried but she wasn't really sure why. What did she have to fear, here among the trees, the lake, the sea? Civilisation was the enemy, as Lyall always said. *Uncontrollable Civilisation*. It reaches its black tentacles a little further each day into all that used to be uncorrupted and pure until poor nature, poor so-called *Uncontrollable Nature*, is herself tamed. Dams are built, rivers rerouted, clouds seeded. We have brought low the Cherubims at Eden's east gate, said Lyall, and doused the flaming sword.

For a little while after that Lyall didn't come and Elena stayed away. Then on a warm evening sitting outside she heard footsteps on the track from the road above the house. It was the boy from the supermarket. He was tall, well dressed, his hair spiked with gel. Lyall's not right in the head, he said, you need to be careful. Elena kept her distance. If you come back without the product, she said, then maybe we could talk. The next day the boy did and Elena made a cold drink for them, but they spent more time looking into their glasses than they did at each other. It's just that he's known in town as a crazy, said the boy; it's a free country, sure, but when I told my dad I'd seen you talking to him he said I should come down here to see if you're okay. He drawled, like his dad, and kept his feet apart. So you've been spying on me, said Elena. The boy blushed and looked at the ground. Elena blushed too. When they said goodbye that afternoon it was like small balls of electricity had started popping in the air between them.

What's your name? said Elena. Aaron, said the boy. He continued on up the road.

When Lyall came by the next day to say hello Elena said sorry, she needed some space. She was sure he could understand. Aaron came by later with a box of fruit from the supermarket that would otherwise have been thrown out. He stood there awkwardly, the box on his shoulder. Has he gone? he said. Elena nodded. When she took the box from him their fingers touched and again the electricity popped. Before Aaron left later that day Elena let him kiss her.

These were the last days of summer. Lyall no longer visited. Elena had never felt particularly uncomfortable with him, aside perhaps from that time he'd touched her arm; he was an eccentric, sure, but in a sense so was she. She told Aaron all this, in order to refute him. Aaron didn't care.

Since their first kiss they'd spent every hour after school and all weekend together, kissing, touching, and much more. In the bedroom with the curtains drawn they'd take off each other's clothes, piece by piece, hesitating and giggling before lying together in the hammock. Some days they would take the hammock outside and string it between two trees and lie in it together, staring and reaching out when the feeling took them to touch. Often in these moments Elena would look down amazed at her own unblemished body, remembering the times in her bedroom at home in front of the mirror when every inch of flesh was covered with a red rash, scratch or weal. Sometimes, remembering, she would stroke her skin with the back of her hand, amazed, even aroused, by its softness.

On one particularly memorable afternoon the pair dragged the old enamel bath out of the shed, set it up on rocks, filled it with the hose and lit a fire beneath. That evening they arranged candles in bottles all around, pushed the coals away, added saucepans of cold water to temper it, then stripped and got in. Elena lay back in Aaron's arms, her white breasts showing above the water. The flickering candlelight threw shadows on the steam, up onto the house nearby, the bush around, the trees above. They were happy. Aaron blew out the candles so that for a moment everything was deep black; when their eyes adjusted there appeared above a sky full of stars and a flock of white gulls drifting past. Birds called from down on the lake, animals talked and skittered in the bush, the waves crashed on the shore. Elena shivered, just for a moment, but Aaron held her tight.

The weather turned, cold wind and rain, and Aaron stopped coming. That had been their summer of love. One night in her hammock Elena was woken by a noise; she lit a candle and as the flame rose up on the wick she thought she saw, briefly, Lyall's face in the window. But it might have been the shadows.

The next day, with a towel held over her head, she traipsed through the wet bush to see him; the drops spitting off the leaves, water splashing down the gullies. The dog whined, but Lyall wasn't there. She pushed the door and it opened. She looked into the little kitchen alcove, behind the bedroom curtain. Then she realised where she was, what she was doing. A black flutter came to her heart. She turned to go and as she did she heard the crunch of leaves and twigs outside. The dog didn't whine—in fact, it seemed all the animals had gone quiet.

Aaron's father told the police he thought they'd run away. Aaron liked the girl, he said, and had been spending a lot of time with her. The police recorded them as missing. But then shortly after a walker found Aaron's battered body washed up on the beach out of town. A couple more days' searching and the cops found Elena's body in a shallow grave in the bush. The dead dog was still on its chain, black liquid oozing from its mouth. It took the police a while to piece it all together and to track Lyall down to his hideout near Ballina on the northern New South Wales coast. The autopsy dated Elena's death to the day, more or less, that an elderly couple saw Lyall's old station wagon speeding out of town.

Sorry it was so sad, said Hannah, I'd forgotten how sad it was. It was all that talk about getting away that made me think of it and then, Lauren, your story—and yours too, Marshall, about Tilly's uncle. But I didn't think through how creepy and sad it all was.

Did all that really happen? said Evan. What do you mean? said Hannah. She's told me that story before, said Leon, unless she made it up then too. It sounded true to me, said Adam, the bit about the allergist especially. I agree, said Marshall. I believed it, said Lauren.

Hannah rested the stick on the arm of the chair. Marshall poured the wine.

Should we do another one? he said. Maybe we should

leave it till tomorrow, said Lauren. There's tiramisu in the fridge, said Hannah. Yum, said Leon. Everyone started stretching and standing up.

Tilly's still in the car, said Evan. He was standing at the window, looking down. Marshall? Tilly's still in the car. I'll go and see what she wants to do, said Marshall. He drank his wine, hitched up his pants.

Sorry everyone, said Hannah; I'm sure I had a happier one there somewhere but that was the one that came out. Lauren and Hannah went into the kitchen. Adam? said Leon, from the couch. Adam was staring at his hands. Marshall's down there now, said Evan; he's trying to talk her in. She's weird, that kid. Evan sat down. I feel like getting absolutely shit-faced tonight: no reason, I just do.

Lauren and Hannah returned, each carrying a tray. One had little bowls and spoons on it, the other the dish of tiramisu with a serving spoon sticking out. They put them both on the table. Tea? Coffee? said Hannah. More wine! said Evan, and everyone except Megan laughed.

Marshall came back up the stairs. He stood there, not moving. She said she won't sleep in the same room as me, he said. Jesus they grow up fast. She can sleep in our room, said Lauren; Adam can go on the couch. You can try, said Marshall. She's upset, said Megan. Lauren stood up. Maybe I should go down and see? There was a pause. Sure, said Marshall. Lauren went down. Tiramisu! said Marshall, picking up one of the little bowls. Everyone, come on, this looks great: tiramisu! They all began helping themselves to the dessert.

Evan came back from the kitchen with another bottle of wine and a fresh San Pellegrino for Leon. The uncle's cottage, he said, I think I know where that is. You sit on that property another five years, a bit of maintenance, keep the grass down, pay the rates and you'd get four hundred grand minimum, and that's on a bad day. The coast here's stuffed; that's pristine property out that way.

Lauren had come back up the stairs. She wants to sleep in the car, she said. I've given her a couple of blankets, she can use the toilet downstairs. I'm going to make her a toasted-cheese sandwich. She hesitated, waiting for Marshall's objection. He had a spoonful of tiramisu. Lauren went into the kitchen. They all listened to her opening the cupboard, taking out the sandwich press, opening and closing the fridge.

I think I might hit the sack, said Megan. Me too, said Hannah. Me three, said Leon. I might stay up for a bit, said Adam. I'll be there soon, said Evan, giving himself a splash of wine. There's sheets and blankets downstairs, said Megan, goodnight. Night all, said Leon. That was good, wasn't it? said Hannah. They went off to bed.

All right, said Marshall, and he sculled his glass. Lauren came back out of the kitchen with a toasted sandwich and went downstairs again. Marshall wasn't sure what to do. All right, he said, go easy men.

They listened to his footsteps going down. Adam? said Evan, holding out the bottle. Half, said Adam. Lauren came back up. Close the fire door, she said, and she walked down the hallway to the bedroom. Adam gave her a late salute.

I think you're right about having themes, he said, pushing a couple more logs into the fire and closing the door. I should go too, said Evan. Megan's going to give it to me otherwise. Adam took his wine outside.

The balcony was new, architect-designed (Evan was right, the house was a hotchpotch of old and new). There was a barbecue with a rain cover to one side and an outdoor dining setting with an umbrella folded down on the other. A hard-wood handrail, with seven tensioned steel cables beneath. Adam walked to where the apex pointed at the sea. The night was still. There were no stars. A moonglow shimmered on the water. A white gull, lost-looking, flew low across the patch of light and off again into the dark. He could see the shape of a suit jacket against the back window of Marshall's car and a silver light inside. It took him a while to realise it was the glow from Tilly's phone.

When he came back in, Evan was still on the couch. I thought you were going to bed? Fuck it, said Evan. Is she asleep? Adam shrugged. That balcony, he said, I tell you— twenty, thirty years of sea air man and, bang, down she comes. It's built all wrong. Concrete cancer. Metal fatigue. It all comes back to bite. Asbestos. He drank. I can't believe he brought her down like that—I mean, what sort of dick does that? This weekend's going to go to shit, I can just feel it. He topped his glass. How are you and Lauren? We're good, said Adam, we're okay. Me and Megan too. A log collapsed in the fire, blowing showers of orange sparks against the glass.

We're a funny species, aren't we? said Evan. Adam looked at him. God or whoever didn't finish us properly when he put those things between our legs and then, when we do it—man on woman, man on man, woman on woman, whatever—we make cries of pain. Cries of pain, Ad—what's that? The kid puts his ear to the door and that's what he hears, one hurting the other. That Tim guy, said Evan, I felt for him. Did you?

Evan stared at the window.

My daughter, Aria, he said, from my first marriage, she was not much older than Tilly when she gave me and Kate a whole heap of trouble. I couldn't even begin. It would be wrong to say that's what caused the break-up but, thinking back, it must have had some effect. Do you know what I mean? But it's all for the best, he said, drinking; Megan and I, we're happy, and I get on with her kids, too. And Aria came through it in the end. She's a woman now. And whip-smart too, I can tell you—she runs rings around me.

She was eighteen when it started; a mature eighteen, mind you, when I think about it, but in another way completely childish. At first it was just a few extra piercings, a couple of tats, peroxided hair, then more tats. She started going out with this guy, he'd bought her drinks or something—I don't know—but here's the thing: he was older than her, much older, the same age as me. She was shameless about it, in a way I guess you have to admire. We don't want our kids cowering, do we? Shortly after Aria and this guy started going out she brought him home to meet us. But here's the thing. My daughter Aria's peroxided, tattooed, pierced— outrageous, in every way—while this guy's as straight as a post. Sensible slacks, nice cotton shirt, he's even brought a bunch of flowers for Kate! Evan threw his head back and laughed, as if Aria's boyfriend handing his ex-wife a bunch of flowers was of all the things he'd seen in his life by far the funniest ever.

This guy's name was Cameron, he worked in border security at the airport, a good, upstanding, righteous job. So he had money, and that wouldn't have hurt. (Aria does like having things). But still, and it's hard to say it even now, I could see on that first night when she brought Cameron home that they were in love, those two, really in love. How's that? Huh? There's Kate and me, sitting opposite, making conversation, and all the time we're thinking, Jesus, those two are in love. That night, when he left, he shook my hand at the door and looked me dead in the eye.

Is this a story? said Adam.

No, said Evan, I don't think so. It sounds like a story, said Adam. Maybe you should save it till tomorrow? But I won't feel like telling it tomorrow, said Evan, I've had a few drinks and I feel like telling it now, because of Tilly in the car. And Tim. And Elena. It's spontaneous, can't you see? Well can you at least give it a title? said Adam. *Border Official*, said Evan; I'll call it *Border Official*. Adam handed him the stick.

So, said Evan.

Evan: Border Official...

That's all you want for your kids, isn't it? Happiness? It seems strange to say it but Cameron and Aria made a great couple. They did everything together: breakfasts out, dinners at the coolest restaurants, shopping on Saturdays at the farmers' markets, Sundays a bike ride along the river. (They met at a club but now clubs were beneath them, they were a sensible couple in love.) Aria still had her tats and piercings but in every other way she was straightening herself up to get, if you know what I mean, in alignment with Cameron. He was the yardstick. She'd even developed, almost overnight, a kind of insane love and respect for her parents. She was proud to bring Cameron home and to talk about him—in whispers mostly, with Kate. She'd also bring home little presents for us: a jar of jam, a bag of apples, a silk scarf for Katie, a stylish wine stopper for me. And all the time there was Cameron, shaking my hand, kissing Aria's cheek, smiling his genuine smile.

That went on for about four months, then we started to detect that something was not quite right. My first instinct was to put it down to the fact that Cameron was working shifts. Sometimes he started at three in the morning and didn't get home till lunchtime: by mid-afternoon he was asleep. I did shift work myself when I was young and it does your head in, I can tell you.

My next thought was that maybe the age difference had finally caught up with them. Maybe Aria was hanging out with men her age and Cameron was getting jealous? Or maybe he was putting expectations on her that she couldn't help pushing against? Maybe she'd actually done something, gone back to the club one night and fucked some old school friend? Maybe that look into the distance was her saying: Yes, I did it, and I don't care what you think. Maybe his look was him thinking that he didn't deserve this young woman and sooner or later he'd have to yield to a rival? But, let's face it, the last thing an eighteen-year-old wants in that situation is parental advice. Kate and I became mute observers, tiptoeing around the minefield.

Then one Sunday Cameron and Aria were both visiting and I found myself alone with him in the backyard. It was a warm day, a bright-blue sky. I offered him a beer. We sat opposite each other on the green plastic chairs. It looked right, but it felt wrong. There we were, the same age, old schoolmates maybe, or workmates, each looking into the mirror at his double: a man in his late thirties, moving too quickly towards middle age, thinking about where he was up to in life and looking, let's be honest, a bit too often at the pretty girls. But there was one difference: *One of these men was going out with the other man's daughter.*

I kept pushing this thought down, squeezing it out of my head and burying it in the patch of ground between us. I was trying to concentrate not on our differences but our similarities. Poor Cameron, I thought, he's carrying all this around on his own: isn't it my duty to help? And aren't I well qualified? Same age, similar background. We both know Aria, each in our own way, I as her father, he as her lover: surely we can figure something out?

I asked him what was wrong. He seemed a bit shocked. I had to repeat myself. I mean, what's wrong between you and Aria, I said. I don't want to pry but she is my daughter and you have become part of the family. Kate and I have seen how something's not quite right between you, there's a stand-offishness or a tension, it's making things uncomfortable around here. It's not our business, I know, I said, but—bear with me—I feel that because we are a similar age (we've never talked about this, it's never been mentioned) maybe I could be the person to talk to? I've been around, I said—yes, it was getting embarrassing—and I didn't come down in the last shower. I had my share of women before Kate got pregnant with Aria and during that time I learned a thing or two about them. And she is my daughter, after all. Maybe, Cameron, I said, it is the age difference? I don't want to say this, I said, but they do say a girl looks to marry a man like her father; that's what they say, but really, I said, when it comes down to it, *does she*? Maybe Aria's hitched up with this father-type a bit too early? Maybe she should live a bit first, I mean with people her own age? And if she has done something, I mean, with someone her own age, maybe the best thing is to talk to her about it, openly. Is that what's happened?

Cameron looked at me blankly, though blankly is hardly the right word. Cameron looked emptily through me. He lifted his beer and drank. He stared at a spot on the ground. It's none of that, he said.

Should we open another one? said Evan. I've got this great Clare Valley too. Adam shrugged: it was all the same to him. Evan got up. Ow, he said, holding his back.

Adam opened the fire door and put a couple more logs in. He went to the window. Clouds had covered the moon; in the car below the light was still on. He pulled the curtains closed.

Are you still up? said Megan. She was standing in the hallway in her pyjamas. We'll be finished soon, said Adam. Oh Jesus, she said. Evan was coming back from the kitchen, holding a fresh bottle. Ad and I are just having a bit of a boy's chat, he said; boys only, for boys. She gave no answer. The hallway light went off; and there was silence again. Real silence: no birds, no wind, no waves, not even that background noise of the great surging sea. Everything was silent and still.

Well, said Evan, easing himself back into the cushions and taking the cap off the wine, peace and quiet. He poured them each a glass. Neither mentioned Tilly or the light below.

So—where was I? said Evan. Yes, there we were, me crapping on about women and fathers and daughters and Cameron was telling me I didn't know shit. It's to do with my job, he said. I asked what he meant. He said it was complicated. I said it was up to him but I was here to listen. He thought about that (*Should I be telling my girlfriend's father this?*) until finally he said, again, almost defeated: It's really very complicated. I waited. Aria and I have had a disagreement, he said, looking up, about something that happened to me at work. Telling you about this isn't the problem, he said, it's telling you why Aria and I disagreed. I didn't follow. Why don't you just start, I said.

I work at the airport, he said, as you know, I've worked there for years and, as you can imagine, there's always been pressure to keep the undesirables out. But then a few years ago, I mean after the terrorist thing, the pressure increased. It is our job to keep our borders safe; nothing more, nothing less. The navy guys up north do their job and we do ours.

A border's not a gateway, it's a fence, with a very small gap cut into it: I can't tell you how many directives come down from on high about the importance of vigilance in the protection of that gap. Emails, memos, in-service training—one bad apple will spoil the whole barrow, they say. Look sharp, be suspicious, never believe what you're told. It is a heavy responsibility and we all feel it, from the minute we put on our uniforms at the start of a shift to when we take them off at the end. And then, on top of that, they decide to make a TV show about us. I looked at him. He raised his eyebrows. Yes, he said, a TV show.

So that was the situation, continued Cameron, when one morning a bit over a month ago near the end of a long Friday-night shift, this incident happened. Let me explain. There'd been a huge influx of Afghanis, I mean after the big NATO surge. Lots had been supporters of the Coalition— drivers, interpreters and so on—but lots more were illegals. Everyone who hadn't visibly fought against us was assumed by the Taliban to have been fighting *with* us and there was now a mighty rush to get out. A crazy time. And it was our job to sort the wheat from the chaff. I'd been out late with Aria almost every night that week and by four in the morning at the end of an insanely busy shift I was wrecked. The TV crew had been following my team all week and this shift they were specifically following me.

Three quarters of cyberspace would disappear if you

took away the vanity, wouldn't it? Point a camera at us and we'll perform. Look at Aria and her friends. And that's the way it was for me: I couldn't turn in any direction that night without a camera and a boom mike somewhere around. Act natural, they said, but acting natural's still acting, isn't it? And with the camera always in my face I found myself acting out what I thought was natural while also feeling—how can I explain it?—that it was not *me* in my body but *me in the camera*, watching me act. Do you know what I mean? I was acting like Cameron, the border security official, the way he, the other Cameron, imagined he should.

Late in the shift a family came through: a couple, mid-thirties, and their three kids, the oldest a girl in her teens. The man claimed to have been a driver for a detachment in Uruzgan and had a letter on army letterhead signed by someone called Captain Smith. I believed it to be a fake. We put the family in the interview room while I searched the database for Captain Smith. I found no such serving member. I told the Afghani male—his English was good, he shook his head—then asked why they had travelled here? He said they had family. I must have looked impressive, doing the US cop-show routine. The crew were happy with the footage. I brought in my superior and briefed him (unbelievably, he didn't double-check the Captain Smith thing) and he agreed the family were illegal and would need to be put on the next available flight out. The Afghani man pleaded, cried, hit his head with his hands; the wife and kids were crying too. Please, please, he said, they will kill me. Late the following afternoon, while I was in bed asleep, they escorted them onto the plane.

It was a few weeks later that I heard the news: the man and his family had only been back two days when they were gunned down in their house. Only Hasti the fifteen-year-old girl survived by hiding under the other bodies and playing dead. It was on the front page, part of a series the paper was doing on the aftermath of the surge; the reporter on the ground had investigated and found the family had been sent back in error. The man—his name was Mehrzad—*was* a driver and Captain Smith, the leader of the forward detachment for which he worked, *had* written a letter for him. Accompanying this article was a photo of the surviving daughter, dressed traditionally, looking off-camera, a backdrop of village roofs and rugged, snow-capped peaks.

It was an awful feeling; I'd never felt anything like it before. I couldn't sleep. I kept seeing that picture in my head of the family being shot (the article said they'd been pushed with rifle butts into a room at the back of the house and mown down with a machine gun), of them cowering in the corner, of the young girl opening her eyes after the killers had gone and realising she was the only one alive.

The doctor gave me sleeping pills. They helped, but they also left me so washed out I hardly ever got up before midday. Aria started getting cranky with me—you asked me what was wrong so I'm telling—and yelling at me to snap out of it. (If only I could!) To her my guilt—guilt that was literally making me sick—was misguided. What are you fretting for, she'd say, you did nothing wrong, those people might have been terrorists, they could have been plotting some suicide attack or something; you sent them back, you were doing your job, why should you feel guilty? I tried to explain that it wasn't that simple, that I had every right to feel guilty, I'd made a mistake that had cost the lives of four people, including two little kids. But Aria wasn't listening. She was thinking about the new nail polish, the new dress her friend had bought, the new shoes for Saturday night.

I'm sorry, I said, said Evan, but I've got to stop you there: we are talking about my daughter, after all. I mean, I know she's got her faults and that but, listen, I'm going to be straight with you, Cameron, I don't get it. You and her, I don't get it. Cameron looked at the ground. Neither do I, he said. He looked up. I bought her a drink, that's all. I was there with a couple of mates; she came up to me and we chatted. It's hard to talk about it, but there *was* a connection, even on that first night, and it never really went away. Not, at least, until now.

So anyway, he continued, Aria and I stopped seeing each other for a while. We still talked—calls, texts, screaming Skypes—but your daughter's opinion was fixed. I had done the right thing, I was being stupid, I should get back to work. I argued back. Like the rest of her generation, I said, she was being selfish, *a selfish bitch*. A family had been killed, just because it happened on the other side of the world didn't make those deaths any less tragic. And to say I was somehow not responsible was to draw a big lie over the facts. I sent her the picture of Hasti, from the paper—the green eyes, the sad stare, the snow-capped mountains behind—and asked did she feel nothing?

So, said Cameron, that's what's been happening. He leaned back and sipped his beer. (The women had left us alone, though at one point I did see Kate come to the back door and watch.) You asked, said Cameron, looking at me, I wouldn't be telling you otherwise. I had a conscience, your daughter didn't. Simple. But—he dropped his head, stared at the back of his hands, jiggled his knees—I love her, Evan, that's the trouble. I love her. A lot.

His voice was wavering. I didn't know where to look. He was whimpering over his love for my daughter! And then, he said, raising his head and shaking it like he was shaking away all those bad thoughts, a few days ago I called Aria and told her that I was making plans to try and sponsor Hasti, the Afghani girl, that there was no other way of dealing with this thing, that I didn't care what she thought and if it meant the end of our relationship, well, so be it. She thought the idea was ludicrous. We argued. Then this morning she rang and asked would I like to come here for lunch. But something was up, I knew. She'd been talking to her friends, I was sure, and was working to a strategy they'd figured out for her: don't dump him yet, you have things on lay-by, a credit card debt, you owe money on your phone. Just before we got here in the car today, I laid out this theory to her, how I believed she was playing a game. She said yes, it was true, she planned to spill the beans in front of you and Kate about this Afghani orphan thing and my pathetic attempt to make myself look important. I had become an embarrassment to her. She said again how she thought it was ludicrous. She looked so young, stupid, naïve.

Cameron was staring at me now, said Evan. I didn't know what to say. Thankfully, just then, Kate called us in to eat.

Adam looked at his watch. Maybe you could skip through it a bit, he said, so we're not still here at dawn? Yeah, maybe, said Evan.

Well, as you can imagine, he continued, the relationship deteriorated pretty quickly after that. She tried to hang on to him for a while, but Cameron saw through it. One day she came home all haughty-looking, her nose in the air, and we both knew it was over. Within a week, she was going out with this guy called Justin, a student, same age, good-looking; he did weekends in a carwash and drove his parents' four-wheel drive.

But, said Evan, *I couldn't get Cameron out of my head.*

I went to see him. He lived out near the airport, in a unit off Taylors Road. He answered the door in his tracksuit and slippers, unshaven, dishevelled and sort of distracted; when he saw me he turned around and walked straight back down the hallway to the kitchen. He'd lost his job, this was the first thing he told me; after the incident with the Afghani family he hadn't been able to cope, always thinking he might make another mistake. He'd even started to doubt the value of the job itself. Why were we sending these people back? Didn't we have enough space? Throw open the doors! Let them all in! He took a payout but the money was going fast. I said maybe I could find him something—I knew a bloke, an old mate of mine, subcontracting on the stations being built on a new railway line out through the north-eastern suburbs. I could put in a good word. It would be physical work, I said, mostly, but good pay. Nine months at least and it could lead to more.

Cameron's reaction was lukewarm. He said thanks, yes, he'd consider. I said how sometimes work is the best way to get us out of ourselves and that moping around all day on your own can't be a good thing. (*My daughter's ex-lover!*) Maybe he should have a think about it? I'll ring Jonno, I said, have a chat, you could even start next week. You need to put all that other stuff behind you, you can't change it now. Then he dropped the bombshell. He was in the process, he said, of seeking permission not to sponsor but to *adopt*. Nothing else would reconcile him to a past that now, he said, shivering slightly, had stuck to him like black glue. I am going to become Hasti's father.

The guy was a fruitcake. I should have left him alone. (And didn't Kate let me know about it after!) But who was I to say he was wrong? And compared to my shallow, skin-and-clothes daughter, to my mind Cameron was the only one who had come out of this relationship with his integrity intact. At least he was *feeling something*.

So I rang Jonno. Cameron started the following Monday. He helped mix cement, cart bricks and tiles, tidy up. Hard work, but hardly taxing on the brain. Jonno said Cameron seemed a bit *noncommittal*, whatever that meant, but he was happy to do me the favour. I didn't tell him he was my daughter's ex. Then one day Jonno rings to tell me the government has put the new rail line on hold. Everyone's laid off, he says; I'm sorry, mate, but I can't worry any more about your hazy friend. I've got a multi-million dollar contract in dispute, they've pulled the pin on the whole thing, there are three half-built stations out there and a line going nowhere. I took the day off work and went round to Cameron's place. He was at the computer. *What was I doing?*

I said I'd spoken to Jonno and if Cameron needed I could help him out for a bit but I was sure he could find something if he put his mind to it. He said he didn't have time to look for work, this was his work now. That night when Aria came home I told her how I'd seen Cameron that day, by chance, that he didn't look happy and maybe she should give him a call? She went berserk, screamed at me, called in Kate and said I was an interfering freak and could she (Kate) please tell me that she (Aria) was not speaking to me ever again unless I got the idea out of my head that she (Aria) might somehow get back with that paedo-creep who actually she would be very happy to see dead? Kate tried to calm her down and the conversation (argument) went on between them for hours, barrelling out through the door of Aria's room. I got a beer and took it outside—the night was warm, the sky full of stars—and started wondering again what on earth I was doing. When Kate came outside later she gave me her lecture (all pretty standard). I agree, I said, I'll stop, I said, I promise.

But I didn't. Why shouldn't Cameron adopt the Afghani girl, give her a new life, make recompense, somehow, for his awful mistake? I shuffled some money around, opened a new account, then secretly sent him a bank cheque every fortnight for roughly what he would have earned if he'd been working. I asked no questions, nor did he.

Time passed. I tried hard to avoid contact with him. But one night he rang me; I had to take the phone outside. He was all bubbly, up. He said—*my God!*—how since we last spoke he'd been writing to the surviving relatives of the girl and how, if he walked in the true way, they'd said, and paid sufficient dowry, there would be no impediment to him taking Hasti as his bride. *What?* There was nothing perverse about

78

it, he said, it was the only way to subvert the authorities, save the girl, and put his conscience to rest. Would I lend him the airfare?

Would I lend him the airfare? Do you hear me? Adam? My daughter's ex-lover, *the man who put his cock inside her, the man whose cock she probably took into her mouth*, this weird freakoid ex-border official was asking would I lend him money so he could go to Afghanistan and marry a fifteen-year-old girl! I said yes. He went. He stayed a year, married Hasti, and brought her home. He got a factory job; they rented a house in Doveton. The last I heard they're still there now.

Evan went silent.

No-one ever knew I helped him. But something went awry in our house. A dark energy came down. Kate and I couldn't stop arguing. Aria became estranged. Then I met Megan—she'd just separated, I was doing her new kitchen— and it seemed right: an older woman, smart, with depth. Depth and feeling. I put all that other stuff behind me, the whole fucking crazy thing.

Evan looked at his watch. Oh Christ, he said. He dragged himself up off the couch. So, yeah, anyway, there it is, that's what happened, go figure.

He walked off down the hallway, the bathroom light went on. Adam could hear him pissing, then the toilet flush. He went to the window and parted the curtains. Yes, Tilly was asleep. The bathroom light went out. Adam damped down the fire and turned off the other lights. In the bedroom he quietly closed the door.

Turn the light on, said Lauren. He couldn't find the switch; she turned on her bedside lamp. Is she still awake? She's sleeping now, he said. It's not right, said Lauren, lying down again. What? said Adam. Everything, she said. She's upset, she's not sleeping out there because she feels like a little camping holiday. Stay out of it, said Adam, taking off his clothes, you can't interfere with stuff like that. Her uncle's just topped himself. Marshall shouldn't have brought her, sure, but we don't know the circumstances. And you know what Jackie's like, she's not exactly Zen Mother.

That girl's upset, said Lauren, that's all I'm saying. She'll be all right tomorrow, said Adam, she'll be hungry, she'll be tired. They both lay looking at the ceiling.

What were you talking about? asked Lauren. Just crap, he said. She turned off the lamp.

There's something a bit sad about us, isn't there? said Adam. Us? said Lauren. I mean how we've only ever danced across the surface, had everything our own way, free education, free dole; no wars, no revolutions. We've not lived to the limit of human experience, we've moved in a little circle. We've looked out for ourselves, not others, and if we do make some big magnanimous gesture there's always something a bit calculated about it. Even when we're listening to another person's cares and woes, aren't we actually thinking about ourselves?

Stop talking, she said, and she rolled over and pulled the covers up to her chin. We're pragmatists, said Adam, idealism's not our thing. No, said Lauren.

Adam lay listening to the sea.

SATURDAY

When Adam woke, fuzzy from the wine, Lauren was already up. So was everyone, by the sounds of it. He went into the kitchen. Megan was at the sink, still in her pyjamas, a pair of ridiculously fluffy slippers on her feet.

She's gone with Hannah and Leon for a walk down the shops. How did you sleep? Good, said Adam, good—is Tilly still in the car? Megan nodded. And Evan? What a night, he said. Megan continued rinsing the dishes. And you? I slept okay, she said. I kept getting all these images, said Adam, not really dreams but the stuff that comes to you when you're sort of skating across the surface. Hannah's story, especially, I couldn't get it out of my head. Do you think it was true?

It sounded true, said Megan.

True's a funny word, isn't it? Have you got a story?

I think so, yeah, and you?

Yeah, I think I've got something.

They heard a toilet flush.

Fuck me, said Evan, walking in—Megan, honey, what were you thinking, telling me to drink all that wine? Where did you get that idea from? He was hugging her from behind; she kept looking out at the rain falling on the stand of acacia trees on the hill behind the house.

You're a fuckin' alcoholic, Evan, honestly, she said. He turned to Adam and widened his eyes. But she still loves me, doesn't she? He buried his face in her neck. Fuck off, she said. Adam opened the fridge and took out a carton of juice. Me too, said Evan. He poured them both a glass. They leaned on the bench and drank. A flock of rosellas screeched and landed in a flurry of wings.

That story did my head in, said Evan. Sweet innocent hippie, then out of nowhere she's telling us about some grue-some murder. I mean, what the fuck was that? Do you think that one had a moral to it? said Adam. About that girl being allergic, to her house, her parents, her life. Could those allergies, multiple chemical sensitivity and all that, chronic fatigue—could they, *quod vide* Sontag, be metaphors? They're clinical conditions, Adam, said Megan, I think that's been pretty well established; sadly what that girl in Hannah's story didn't have was proper professional and parental support.

Evan gave Adam his cartoon look again. And you can fuck off, said Megan, without looking at him. Everything with you guys is always so cynical, isn't it? She turned back to the sink, closed the dishwasher and turned it on. Evan did his look again—a watered-down, furtive version—and took his glass of orange juice out into the living room.

Morning all! said Marshall. He was dressed, his hair wet and combed; he must have used the shower downstairs. He poured himself a juice. Tilly's got herself a cup of tea, he said. I took it down earlier, said Megan. That seemed to deflate Marshall; he didn't know what to do with his hands. So what's to eat? he said.

The walking party came back upstairs.

Breakfast's here! said Hannah. Free-range eggs, organic bacon, sourdough bread, freshly squeezed orange juice and special sweetie treats for later! They were all wearing hats and coats and scarves. Leon was last up, carrying the papers. Did you find some umbrellas? said Megan. It was nice in the rain, said Lauren, the air's beautiful out there. Leon's got a story, said Hannah. Lee?

They started taking off their things and hanging them over the chairs near the fire. Everything smelled faintly of the sea. Lauren took a pebble from her pocket and put it in Adam's hand. She smiled, a big smile, maybe a false smile, but a loving smile too. He kissed her cheek—it was getting warmer—and put the pebble in his pocket. Lauren turned to Marshall. Tilly's got herself a cup of tea, she said. Marshall? Tilly's got herself a cup of tea.

There was a piercing noise. What the fuck is that? said

Evan, holding his hands out away from his ears, ready to clamp them down. It's the fire alarm, said Marshall, the fire alarm's gone off. Is there smoke? Did someone burn something? Marshall had only just finished yelling when the fire alarm in the living room stopped as quickly as it had started. There was silence again, aside from the rain on the roof and the water gurgling in the pipes. Well thank Christ for that, said Evan. Is there smoke? said Marshall, looking around. Can anyone smell smoke?

They set the dining-room table, got the breakfast ready. They made a good team. There were lots of jokes and banter, light-hearted arguments about the best way to do this and that, whether there should be milk in the scrambled eggs, whether the toast should be light or dark, whether there should be oil in the pan before you fry the bacon. Adam laid the cutlery; Lauren brought the warm plates out. In a low voice she told him how when they'd come up the driveway and passed Tilly in the car with her cup of tea they'd heard her phone go *ping*.

I heard it too, said Leon, from behind. He was carrying a big plate of bacon. Hannah was behind him with the scrambled eggs. Me too, she said. What are you talking about? said Marshall, with a jug of juice. Tilly's phone, said Adam. We made a pact, said Megan, putting the plunger of coffee down. Come on people, really, she said, it's only a couple of days. I should check in with Jackie though, said Marshall. No-one knew what to say to that. They all sat down to breakfast.

If it's something important she'll ring on Tilly's phone, won't she? said Megan. Everyone started serving themselves from the spread. The downstairs shower went on. Marshall speared a piece of bacon and pretended not to hear.

Did you see this? said Leon, flicking the paper flat, someone's just paid thirty thousand for what they say are Ned Kelly's long johns. There's even a certificate of authenticity. How do you certify someone's undies? said Evan. I didn't think we were allowed papers, said Adam. A private collector bought them. Good for them, said Lauren. *I am a widows son outlawed*, said Leon, *and my orders must be obeyed*. Can I have real estate? said Evan. There was a sudden scream in the pipes. And sport. That's ridiculous, said Lauren, how can the value of something like that get measured in dollars? What else are we going to measure things in? said Marshall. Love units? The downstairs shower stopped. I might take down a plate, said Megan. A while ago, said Adam, following his own thread, they found a piece of surveying equipment from the Burke and Wills expedition and that fetched a lot of money too. I guess we're a bit desperate to fill the artefacts cupboard, aren't we? With the stories of losers, said Megan.

She took the plate downstairs.

That's great bread, said Evan, holding up a slice. Is that sourdough?

Sometimes, said Hannah, in a good bakery, they might

use the same starter for decades. What? said Evan. The yeast, said Hannah, in sourdough. As long as it's kept warm and moist it continues to be active, so the baker takes a bit of the dough they've used to make that morning's batch, adds a bit of flour and puts it aside in a warm place and when they fold it into the next day's dough it acts as a starter to make the dough rise, then from that you take another bit and that's the starter for the next day and so on. Jesus, said Marshall. Just like, said Adam. And generally, said Hannah, the older the starter the better the bread. Evan flicked the paper. Bread's ridiculous, he said. What? said Lauren. The price, said Evan, it's flour and water for chrissakes.

Megan came back up the stairs, sat at the table and resumed eating.

Listen to this, said Evan. Four bedroom, architect-designed with sea views, large living area, rain tanks, grey-water recycling, sloping bush block, five mins beach and shops. How much? One point five, said Marshall. A million, said Lauren. Two million, said Leon. Megan? Nine hundred thousand. The same, said Hannah. Adam? Two oxen and a sheaf of barley. Two point five, said Evan. No way, said Marshall. Yes way, said Evan. That's crazy, said Megan. Two and a half million, said Hannah, for a holiday house? But you could live down here, said Evan, it's a family home. But where would you work, what work would you do? There's work in Geelong. But two point five million? You sell that inner-suburban home, said Evan, and you've got money to spare.

How long's it been on the market? said Marshall. Doesn't say, said Evan.

A friend of ours, said Hannah—well, not really a friend, someone we know—bought a house in Daylesford last year for just under two million. Nice garden and all that but nothing special. What worries me, said Lauren, in that situation, is that you sell in the city and buy in the country but if you don't like it and you want to go back to the city later, well, you can't, can you? You can't afford to. It's a one-way street. I'd be offering one point seven tops.

Here's another one, said Evan: one point six. Three bedroom, period, edge of town, established garden, circular drive, double garage, five mins walk to beach. Doesn't sound like anything special though, does it? said Lauren. You'd need to have a look, said Marshall. It's nearly a million dollars cheaper, said Hannah. I'd have it, said Adam. In your dreams, said Lauren. Best place to be, said Adam. I just think that's fucking outrageous, said Megan, that people are prepared to pay that much for a house down the beach. It'd be nice though, Meg, wouldn't it? said Lauren. Sure, said Megan, but still. Lee, said Evan, how much did you pay for Halls Gap? Two hundred for the land, said Leon, and sixty to build. It's beautiful up there, said Hannah. The coast's a better investment though, said Evan, it's always going to hold its price better than the bush.

The conversation fizzled out. The table was cleared, the dishwasher stacked. Lauren cut up some vegetables and got them on the stove so they could have soup later. Leon and Marshall made themselves a second coffee; Megan and Evan sat in the living room browsing the papers. It was nice inside, with the fire going and the rain pattering on the roof and the sound of waves flopping down there on the shore. Adam went to the toilet, Lauren to the shower. Hannah shook the table-cloth off the edge of the balcony and when she came back in she had raindrops, like pearls, in her hair.

Brr, she said.

Lauren returned with her hair in a towel. Adam was carrying a book. Everybody, look, *Future Shock*! he said. There was a rumble of thunder. The air turned cold and metallic. Hannah knelt up on a chair to see.

Is everyone comfortable? said Megan. She handed Leon the stick. You'll need to speak up, said Evan. Is she okay out there? asked Hannah. Marshall nodded.

So, said Leon—everybody?—my story is a true story that might end up sounding like it isn't. But it all happened. The basis of it, he continued, has a bit to do with what's going on here, I mean how much truth we tell each other, even friends, and how many lies. It's about the death of idealism, too— Jesus, said Evan—and the growth of expediency. It's about someone trying to dig down to the core of things, to get at some truth, but who feels like he's digging through a pile of feathers to nothing.

Do you remember that guy from uni who was in that student production? Adam? *Three Sisters*. Remember? You were Solyony. Marshall, you were Tuzenbakh. I was Kulygin. He was Vershinin. Lauren, you were Masha. *In two or three hundred years life on earth will be inexpressibly beautiful and amazing.* His name was Aiden. He was involved in student politics too—Marshall, remember?—and he used to hand out flyers and all that. I lost touch with him after we graduated but then one day, around 2005—maybe 2006—I bumped into him in the city.

He hadn't aged well: bald on top, long white hair, a beard, scruffy clothes and some kind of skin disease, like a bad case of acne. It felt awkward, I won't lie. He asked did I want a drink. Come on, he said, for old times. We went into the front bar of Young and Jacksons. It wasn't like drinking in the daytime was an unusual thing for me back then. It was three in the afternoon and still pretty quiet. I offered to shout. No, he said, and he pulled out a wallet with a wad of bills.

Leon: The Broken String...

We went and sat at one of those high tables on a couple of stools near the window. He asked what I'd been up to and I told him how I'd knocked around for a while after getting my BA, went into journalism, travelled, wrote, married, divorced, married and divorced again. He looked interested, for a moment, then he stared into his glass. I was already wishing I'd said no. He said he'd moved to Canberra and enrolled in post-grad politics at ANU; he just couldn't connect with the old crowd. He became a student again, did student things. He met a diplomat's daughter and they got married and had a kid. Then he dropped out and took a bureaucratic job, advising government, boring as all hell, in a place called the Office of National Assessments.

But, said Aiden, what could I do? I had a wife, a kid, a mortgage. Canberra had just sort of sucked me down. We had another kid. Then, about eight years ago, late nineties, for various reasons that I won't go into here but let me say involved a story about so-called illegals drowning or *not* drowning at sea, I took stress leave. At first I just pottered around the garden, played in the shed, dabbled in carpentry, looked up at Mount Ainslie, thinking nothing. I usually had my first beer around three. I also started revisiting the campus, on the side, wandering around, eating my lunch. I was thirty-two, going on thirty-three. My wife, Lil, was worried, I know, but she couldn't fix things for me. So one day I left, just like that; yes, I packed a bag and took the bus back to Melbourne. I don't know what came over me, really, but I know I was telling myself that I was not running away from things but *into* them. Do you know what I mean?

I got a room off the board at Readings, a shitty room in a

sharehouse up the shitty end of Coburg. My housemates were all younger, early to mid-twenties, as was just about everyone I hung around with in those years. I worked odd jobs: tele-marketing, delivery driving, dishpigging, and sent what money I could back to Lil. It was never much. What was I doing? I didn't know. But I was sure I had to keep doing it, like when you're running downhill and if you don't keep going you fall.

With the people in the house—all students—I started gravitating back to the stuff I'd been into before; politics, I mean. I started hanging around Trades Hall, the New International Bookshop, going to meetings, demos. I bought myself a Lenin cap (it covered up my bald patch) and got back into theatre, amateur stuff mostly, not very good, but I loved the camaraderie of it. And at least what we were doing had an edge, at least it was *about something*. That's what I told myself, anyway. The beginning of 2000. A good time. Actually, every-thing felt good.

Aiden got off his stool. He asked did I want another and came back this time with a jug. Why not? he said.

Well, the next part, said Aiden, raising his beer, starts with an image I can't get out of my head: my Lenin cap lying in a puddle in a lane behind the Crown Casino on the twelfth of September 2000. The World Economic Forum. A cop had just punched me in the head. I'd been hanging around all day with my housemates—a pretty ineffectual bunch, really—when I thought I might wander off and see what was going on elsewhere. I've always been doing that, wandering off. I walked all the way around the blockade and back out onto the Spencer Street Bridge where I saw a group pointing and shouting. A police barge was ferrying delegates up the river from the hotel on the other side. Someone yelled: *Down here!* and everyone started running towards the voice. Without thinking, I ran down there too.

The lane below the bridge was empty. *Buses here! Buses here!* someone yelled. In the loading dock behind the hotel were three big touring buses with a queue of men in suits getting onto the first. They were going to try and break the line. *Stop the buses! Stop the buses!* Everyone ran to the front of the first bus, and, spontaneously—magically, I remember thinking—twenty or so people formed a chain and blocked the door.

The queue of delegates had split when they saw us coming; some ran back to the loading dock with their security guards following, the others madly scrambled up the steps while the driver closed the door. I ended up dead centre, under the front window. There was a young guy, straight-looking, on one side of me and a girl, younger, hippie-looking, on the other. It all happened so quick. I remember the way we smiled at each other when I raised my elbows so they could link arms in mine, as if the three of us were about to set off on a *do-si-do*.

Hold the line! Hold the line! Then everything went

quiet—and that's when the weirdness came down. Twenty-odd people, different ages, male and female, all types, *citizens*, standing around a big touring bus in an ugly city laneway, while there above us, inside, sat about thirty men in suits, citizens too, clutching their briefcases, terror in their eyes, wondering how on earth this had happened. And so it went on, for what felt like an hour but was more likely a couple of minutes. The chanting stopped, then the murmuring started. *Hold the line—Arms linked—Don't be scared—You have the right to protest—Look at their badges, get their names—Don't speak without a lawyer—Are you okay up front?—Is everybody ready?—All right, hold the line.* I turned to look at the girl next to me and saw how her eyes had glazed over. Don't be scared, I said. She smiled, a half-smile, squeezed out through the fear. A beautiful smile, I'll never forget it. Thanks, she said. We looked straight ahead again and I could feel her link her arm in mine a little tighter.

Then we heard it.

It was a phalanx of cops in riot gear: dark-blue boiler suits, pants tucked into knee-high boots, helmets, batons. They weren't trotting, they were running. It took them a while to assemble into a solid line and start the dance-chant that had been going on everywhere in the streets that morning. *Move! Move!* they shouted (it sounded like they were saying *Moo!*) and in rhythm with the chanting they stomped forward, step by step. They started the dance about ten or fifteen metres away—me, the guy to my left, the girl to my right, the only ones facing them directly, we all stiffened. Then with each chant, they moved closer. Chant, shuffle, chant. The protesters behind us started chanting back, trying to drown them out: *The whole world's watching! The whole world's watching!* The cops upped the volume: *Move! Move! Move!* It took a while for us to see the whites of their eyes. The cop directly in front of me had locked on: I was his target, little old me, with my cute little Lenin cap. I could sense the fear running through the girl's arm into mine. So this is what it's like, we were thinking, to put your ideals on the line. We want a better world, this one's fucked, but all that cop there wants to do is bash the living crap out of us and tell his mates about it after.

Aiden stopped for a moment and stared behind me into the street. He let a thought pass through him.

They were only a few metres away now, he said, and you could feel the line tightening. Then a cop in a different uniform appeared—maybe he'd been hiding behind the others all along? He stepped back into the empty space and put a megaphone to his mouth. *Move away from the bus— Move away from the bus—Move away from the bus and you won't get hurt—Move away from the bus.* Some of us started chanting again: *Hold the line! Hold the line!* The guy with the megaphone started to yell: *This is your last—*but then, from the top of the lane, behind him, there was the sound of running and shouting. It was the same shout as before: *Buses* *here! Buses here!* The cop lowered his megaphone, the others glanced around: a mob of protesters was coming round the corner from the direction of the blockade, led by the anarchists in their boiler suits and masks.

Charge! I heard someone say. *Cops here!* said someone else. *Hold the line!* a protester screamed. Then my cop, the cop with my name written on him, was on top of me. He ripped my arm away from the girl's, twisted it behind my back and whacked me hard a couple of times across the head. Then he threw me aside. As I went down I saw him hoe into the guy next to me, then help another cop pull protesters away from the door.

In a few seconds they had broken the chain but now the second lot of protesters was at their backs fingering the air. *Whose streets?—Our streets!—Whose streets?—Our streets!* The cops turned and it was game on. They charged the frontline, of anarchists mostly. (There'd been stories earlier that these guys were throwing paper bags of shit at the cops near the King Street entrance: this was revenge.) The cops beat a wedge through the anarchists but soon found themselves surrounded. *The world is watching! The world is watching!* I got to my feet and made it to the footpath, away from the action. My head was throbbing, I'd bitten my tongue, I'd lost my hat somewhere in the scuffle. I saw it lying in a puddle in the middle of the road—but then I heard the hooves.

Time slowed down and sped up. The crowd scattered, the

mounted police cleared a path to the bus and behind them came more reinforcements on foot. The lane was cleared, everyone was pushed back to the footpath and beyond. Protesters were running down laneways, cowering in doorways, falling back towards the river. People were bleeding, screaming. The cops on horses ringed the bus while a cordon on foot ushered the delegates out. I remember one businessman shouting over their heads at us: *You fucking scum!*

The bus started up, the cordon tightened, and with the delegates looking out at us—safari tourists inspecting the animals—it drove off down the lane. The cops closed in and swallowed it up and the whole circus moved off to Spencer Street and from there, presumably, towards the main blockade.

I hung around in the lane for a while; most of the others had chased the cops and the bus. Someone who'd seen me get punched asked was I all right and did I need medical attention or want to sign a statement. I said no, I was fine, thanks. The few who were left started drifting away. Then I remembered my hat, lying in the puddle. But it was gone. I heard the girl's voice behind me, the girl whose arm had been linked in mine. I picked it up, she said, but I couldn't find you. She held it out; I took it from her.

Are you okay? I asked. She nodded. And you? Yeah, I said. She had a friend with her, older than her but younger than me, soft-faced, good-looking, a real sincerity about him. She told him who I was, what had happened. I'm Jordan, he said, and he shook my hand. And I'm Rani, she said. She looked at me, then her eyes clouded over. Is it worth it? she said. Yes, I said, I think so, yes.

Well, continued Aiden, of course I felt like a hero. Why not? I was jumpy, I remember, I couldn't settle down. I stayed around the blockade the rest of that day and came back again the next. No-one was getting in or out. Then, before dawn on Monday morning, everything changed again. The riot guys arrived, batons flailing, and attacked the least-protected Queen Street entrance. The protesters, still half-asleep, didn't stand a chance. The cops came in over the top like sheepdogs, bashing as they went. The horses followed behind. After that came the buses, with the faces inside. It was all over in minutes.

For days the airwaves were filled with suggestions about what to do with us scum now that we'd been vanquished— stick our heads on pikes at the city gates, and worse. We melted back into what we'd been doing, which, true, in a fair few cases, probably wasn't much. But I'm sure everyone felt the same, that something had started and was gathering momentum, not just here but everywhere; that it was not just a handful of ferals screaming for change but all kinds of people, like on the blockade, like those who linked arms around the bus, people who had never got off their arses before now getting out and being seen. They'd been name-called and demeaned so many times over the years, by politicians, shock jocks, the patriotic plebs, and now they were standing up. It's one of the bravest things you can do as a human being, isn't it? Refuse to be belittled.

There were more protests that year and into the next: Prague, Davos, Salzburg, Genoa. I got even more heavily involved with all this underground political stuff. I was on a high, I won't deny it. I helped out with websites, wrote press releases, distributed flyers, went to meetings two or three times a week, all the time still washing dishes, cleaning offices, packing boxes or whatever. I spent my spare time online, sharing information and strategies with the other disillusioned around the world, or in the lounge room with my cask wine and juice-bottle bong watching news and current affairs. My housemates joined me in a rotating parade—I think they liked having the crazy older guy around. I read every analysis I could find about the present state of mainstream politics and the more I did the more helpless I felt. The drawbridges had gone up, the ranks had closed; democracy was an impenetrable fortress. You couldn't get at it, it wouldn't let you in. Politicians had become actors, their performances cool steel.

Then one afternoon I rang Lil, to see how she was getting on. It was months since we'd spoken and she sounded estranged. I said again how sorry I was but, please, all the same, could I have a quick word with the kids? She said no. Then I heard a male voice, telling her to tell me to fuck off. Put him on, Lil, please, I said. No, Aiden, she said, you've got no right. I pleaded with her, said I was sorting things out, that I would come through this in the end for sure. Lil listened, then in a voice so cold it almost froze my ear, she said: Aiden, I'm with Niall now.

He was a diplomat's son, same stock as her—a few months later I was back in Canberra for the divorce. What a strange place. Niall was there, of course, but they wouldn't let me near him. My God, Aiden, said Lil, when she saw me: what's happened? It was a long and drawn out bitch fight, naturally, but in the end they gave me half the house if I agreed to stay away from the kids.

Things went off the rails a bit after that. I started drinking more and smoking way too much weed. Most of the settlement money I squirrelled into a high-yield investment account but the rest I started giving away—for good causes, let me say, nothing but good causes. I even helped sponsor a John Pilger tour. Then one evening in early 2001 I was coming out of a meeting in one of the rooms upstairs at Trades Hall when I passed a doorway and saw Jordan inside. Jordan from the demo. He was giving a speech, a politico-philosophical speech. It took me a while to realise he was speaking not as himself but as an actor in a play. There were other actors there too; listening, gesturing, rhubarbing. *They call themselves intelligentsia*, Jordan was saying, *but they're rude to servants, they treat peasants like animals, they are poor students, they read nothing seriously, they don't do a thing.* In the corner a young musician was bending and distorting the notes on an electric guitar. Rani was in there too. Jordan finished speaking and an older guy—shoulder-length hair, three-day growth—started giving him notes. Aiden! said Jordan, when he saw me. They all turned around. Everyone, said Jordan, this is Aiden, the guy who was with Rani at the front of the bus.

It was a rehearsal, they were preparing a show, and instantly all those good feelings I had making student theatre came back. There was something about the smell in the room, the tape on the floor, the props in the corner, the old table with tea and coffee on it, the loose clothes of the actors. Dane, the director, called a break and explained what they were doing. It was *The Cherry Orchard*, in a new mash-up version. I told him I'd done Chekhov at uni. The winds of change are coming, said Dane, theatrically, just the same now as then, and again the self-satisfied bourgeoisie have stopped up their ears and cannot hear it: *as if up in the sky, the sound of a broken string.* He had his hand up, fingers curled, as if about to grab hold of the string.

He was about my age, mid-thirties, a raffish guy with a big personality. He was hard not to like. The plan was to do the show guerrilla-style, one performance only, advertised underground on the networks, on an island (the Ranevskaya estate) in the middle of the Yarra. From the direction of the city, as the show neared its end, we would hear the approaching sounds of the machinery of change—chopping, slashing, grinding—and the looped wail of a broken string.

The front bar of Young and Jacksons was starting to fill. It was just after four. Aiden poured the dregs from the jug. One more? he said.

I was supposed to be back at the office, I had copy to fill, there's no way I should have been drinking like that on a Tuesday afternoon. I watched Aiden take the empty jug back to the bar. Here's my chance, I thought, turn now and run and you could be back at your desk working before he even realises you're gone. But I seemed stuck to the stool.

Well, said Aiden, filling our glasses from the new jug, I suppose you can guess what happens next. With my divorce money I offered to fund Dane's production. It was crazy—and that's exactly why I wanted it to happen. Aside from being its principal investor I helped out generally around the place, making props, doing the lunch runs. I was still living in the Coburg sharehouse, as far as I could possibly be from the Canberra public servant of old.

One morning I headed off on the tram a little earlier than usual and when I got to Trades Hall Rani was sitting on the steps. The others hadn't arrived. We started talking, about the play, mostly. I felt strange, there was a prickle under my skin. She had her hair up; her neck was pale, almost powdery white. That morning we worked on the scene, a tender scene, where the 'perpetual student' Trofimov (Jordan) speaks with young Anya (Rani) and waxes lyrical again: *It's so very clear that to begin to live in the present we must first redeem our past.* We sat around the edges of the space while Dane worked the actors hard, occasionally turning to us and asking for an opinion. At one point he got Rani up and asked her to forget that she was only seventeen and to seduce shamelessly the older, bumbling Trofimov until she had him on the floor. She did as Dane suggested but I could see she wasn't 'in' it. He called a break. *Onward! Don't fall back!* said Jordan, putting a consoling arm around her, and everybody, including Rani, laughed.

That night when I got home I encouraged my house-mates to drink with me, dragging out the bottles I'd kept in my bedroom. I felt strangely free. Come on, one more, I kept saying. I was last into bed—it was well after midnight—still dancing on my thoughts.

The big performance came around pretty quick after that: 21 April, 2001. Over the previous week, each night under the cover of darkness, we had ferried the gear over to the island and set up: generator, lighting, sets, costumes, props. I was among those who slept out there; we laid low, kept quiet, lit no fires, used torches only when we had to. On the night itself— a cool autumn evening and no sign of rain—the audience members gave a gold-coin donation to the boatman before being rowed over six at a time.

It was a good crowd, a full house. They loved it, from the bustle of arrival to the final image of Lopakhin, the freed *muzhik*, taking a petrol-powered whipper snipper to the papier-mâché orchard while the electric guitar screamed and wailed. The cast took three curtain calls. The audience went mad. Dane joined them for the last, taking centre of the line, bending himself into a bow, holding the pause, letting his hair hang, rising and flicking it back.

While the audience were ferried back off the island, the cast and crew stayed on for the party. Four big ice tubs were dragged out into the main performance area and the *doof-doof* started. I went back to the dressing room—a tent behind a stand of trees—to congratulate the actors. Rani had taken off her costume and was sitting in front of the mirror in a skirt and powder-blue bra, the top hook undone, the underarm edging slightly frayed. When my lips brushed her cheek it smelled of perfume, makeup and sweat. Dane handed me a beer. You see! he said. I hung around in the dressing room, listening to them talk, before pushing my way through the bushes to the riverbank on the city side where I sat looking at the lights.

It had been a trip all right, from a public servant with a wife and kids in Canberra just two years before to this. I sat and thought about it. Then I heard a rustle in the bushes behind: it was Rani. The *doof-doof* had grown louder, as had the voices of the people partying back on the grass. Someone's going to ring the cops, she said, sitting down next to me with her cup of wine: do you reckon we could swim from here? She was pointing at the far bank, the freeway above it, the cars whooshing past. She'd bunched her hair up and secured it with pins. The moon was high, a half-moon. *All our fine conversations are just to divert our own and others' attention.*

Everything got mixed up in my mind—I leaned over and asked could I kiss her. She didn't say yes or no but she didn't move away so I took this as a sign. She kissed me back at first, but then I felt a resistance—a resistance, ha! a rebellion! Her lips tightened, she turned away. But I kept going. She was only—what?—ten, twelve years younger. I put an arm around her and pulled her towards me. I kissed her hard. She bit my lip. I pulled back and she started to scream so I put a hand over her mouth. Please, I said. Please. Her eyes were wide. Please, I said, I'm sorry, don't scream. I'll take my hand away but don't scream. She was huffing through her nose, trying to catch her breath. Please don't scream, I said, again. My palm was wet with her spit. I drew it away. She gasped. Please, I'm sorry. I lay down next to her and hugged her close. I was crying, a grown man crying! I'm sorry, I kept saying, I'm sorry.

She got up. It's okay, she said. They were the only words she'd spoken since the whole thing started. Then she turned and hurried away.

The first person I saw when I made my way back was Jordan. He'd come down to the river for a piss. I told him I had to go. But the party's just starting, he said. He picked up the beer he'd pushed down into the grass—he'd already had a few. I told him something had come up, with my ex-wife back in Canberra; I had to leave Melbourne tonight. He said he'd row me back.

He was high on the success of the night and chattered at me all the way back across the island to where the dinghy was tied up. He was still talking when he raised the oars. It worked, didn't it? he was saying. They were with us, weren't they? Aiden? We must look for a deeper truth, beneath all the banging and shouting, we have to see our faults, change ourselves from the inside, before we can expect to change anything in the world.

He was talking madly, rowing badly; the current was moving us downstream. We'd gone at least half the length of the island before we were close enough to the opposite bank for me to throw a rope and lasso a bush. The dinghy pulled up with a jerk. Be careful going back, I said. Jordan waved and smiled. I threw the rope; he turned the dinghy around. The *doof-doof* was fainter, but you could see the glow from the bonfire and hear the voices above the trees. Someone would complain, for sure. I took one last look at Jordan, still in costume as the perpetual student, Trofimov, rowing hard across the current.

The story was, continued Aiden, that the cops raided the party soon after. The water police came in from the city side while three divvy vans covered the other bank. The partygoers were trespassing, they had no permit, they were disturbing the peace, all that. The cops didn't treat them nicely. It was in the middle of all this ruckus that someone realised Jordan was missing.

The dinghy was found next morning downriver, in the shadow of the city, jammed between the bow of a pleasure cruiser and the berth. The body didn't turn up till two days later; it had washed almost out to sea. Because I was the last to see him alive the cops came round to see me. I answered all their questions, said he was drunk and reckless and that there was nothing I could do. The coroner called it death by misadventure—an understatement, if ever there was one.

I went to the funeral. Rani was there. We spoke a few words but didn't touch. I have never felt so sad or bereft. After the service Dane asked was I interested in investing in his new idea: a mash-up version this time of a Dostoevsky novel, about nihilism, revolution, disenchantment, murder. The great disillusionment drowning the world. He pointed out the dramaturg, a tall, skinny guy. They would do it flash-style, he said, in Canberra, on the steps of Parliament House. He pulled the paperback from his pocket and read to me from the scene where the suburb over the river catches fire: *It's all arson! It's nihilism!* Well? Aiden? What do you think?

I said no.

What else could I say? I had left my job, my wife and kids, I had treated a young woman badly and let a young man drown. I had bought a drop of self-importance with a bucketload of spoilt money. What right did I have to an opinion about anything? What entitlement? I woke late the morning after Jordan's funeral with a goon-sack hangover and watched the light seeping through the blanket at the window. What morals do you have, Aiden? I showered and dressed. And without morals what *do* you have? Anything? I made breakfast, sat out in the backyard in the sun. I had a good think. Well, I thought, I've still got money. I've got no responsibilities. I can do what I like. Ah! I said. That's what I've got: freedom. Freedom—what about you?

I moved out of the sharehouse into a city apartment with a view of the river and the bay. I bought the best food, wine, drugs. I hung out with gangsters, pimps. I lived like a king. I spent whole days in the casino (the casino!—ha!) and rented a new girl every night. Sometimes I rented two. Sometimes I got one that looked like Lil, sometimes one like Rani. We always drank the best champagne. Did you ever do it with two? Leon? Three? I've still got cash, he said, pulling it out. Here.

It was at that point, said Leon, that I realised not only that we were both pissed but that we'd slipped down a rabbit hole into another place—a place I quickly realised I didn't want to be. The bar had filled; it was five o'clock and the after-work punters had arrived. Aiden had a crooked smile. So you see? he said. We're fucked, aren't we? Hypocrites. Liars. We've let the whole thing go to shit, and now there's nothing we can do.

Aiden's voice changed then—no, not just his voice, his whole demeanour. He straightened his spine and lifted his chin. He was doing Vershinin. Remember? *Well. Thank you for everything*, he said. *I've talked a great deal, a very great deal—forgive me for that too.* He did the crooked smile. *So, I'll go off by myself*, he said—and then he was gone.

Leon's words just sort of hung there. It was only now in this seeming silence that they realised it was not silent at all. The rain was belting down, falling in sheets, cascading off the balcony and out of the gutters and smattering the big windows every time the wind whipped it sideways. It had built up all morning, and now they were in the middle of a storm.

Shit! said Marshall, heaving himself up off the couch: Tilly's still in the car! That's it, she's coming in.

All this caught everyone by surprise. It was as if the flurry of activity had left a momentary hole in the room. Marshall went down. The soup, said Lauren. She and Megan went into the kitchen. The others listened to the rain.

Shit day for footy, said Evan. Adam nodded. People used to tell the weather by looking at the sky and studying the behaviour of animals, said Hannah. Evan pointed at the window. Rain, he said. A mackerel sky, said Hannah, I love that expression. Is that like when it's raining fish? It's when white clouds in a blue sky look like the markings on the side of a mackerel, said Hannah; they tell us a front is approaching, although it may be a long way off; a mackerel sky may mean rain, but not always. That's handy, said Evan. If cockatoos come down from the mountains to the coast, it's going to rain, she continued; they even say you can tell how many days of rain there will be by how many cockatoos there are. Ants tell you that too, don't they? said Adam. All this will be gone soon, said Leon, because of what's happening to the world.

The blender went on in the kitchen and Marshall came back upstairs. She's not in the car, he said. Lauren came to the kitchen door. She's put my stuff outside the room, and a chair or something up against the inside. She won't speak to me; she won't come out. What's going on? said Megan. She'd come in from the kitchen too. Tilly's moved into the room downstairs, said Hannah. Well thank Christ for that, said Lauren, and she went back to the soup. Maybe I should have a word to her? said Megan. Sure, said Marshall. Megan went downstairs. The fire alarm rang again. Ah for fuck's sake, said Marshall, who'd just sat down. Are you burning something in there? The alarm kept screeching. For fuck's sake! said Evan.

They were all out of their seats now, looking at the ceiling. Evan found a broom and used it to push the button but the alarm didn't stop. What the fuck? said Megan, who'd come back up the stairs. It's faulty, said Leon. Can you stop it? said Megan. We're trying, said Evan. Is there a ladder? said Marshall. He and Evan went to find one while Adam, Leon, Megan and Hannah just stood there, staring up. Lauren came out of the kitchen. Can someone turn that fucking thing off?

The alarm didn't stop, not like last time, it just kept going on and on. Marshall and Evan came back, huffing and puffing and wet from the rain, carrying an aluminium stepladder that they bumbled around with for a while until Evan managed to click the thing into the thing. He held it while Marshall went up. He seemed to take forever to figure out how to open the flap. Then the screeching stopped. Well thank Christ for that, said Lauren, again. Marshall threw the battery down. Have we got a fresh one? asked Hannah. The alarm's broken, said Leon. But what if there *is* a fire? said Hannah. The storm'll put it out, said Evan. Everyone looked at him, trying to figure out if this was a joke. Marshall climbed back down.

The rain was falling just as heavily, but everything seemed calmer after the screech. My ears are ringing, said Evan. Is she okay? said Marshall. Megan didn't answer. Marshall sat on the couch. Soup's ready! said Lauren, from the kitchen. Yum, said Leon. We've got no bread, said Hannah. Did we eat it all? asked Leon. There's some white in the freezer, said Megan. White? said Adam—*white?* I can whiz down, said Evan. Ad, Lee, Marsh: do you want to nip down the shops? You're getting more grog, aren't you? said Megan. Evan shrugged. (He looked like a little boy.) We can take mine, said Marshall, already up, fishing in his pockets for the keys.

The three women listened to the four men going down.

What should we do? said Megan. Nothing, said Lauren, there's nothing we can do. She scares me, that kid, she's so— self-possessed. They listened to the door below close. She's had to be, said Megan, you can't blame her, she's learning how to hold her own, because of Jackie, and what's been happening at home. And now this. They heard Marshall's car reversing, changing gears, fading down the hill. It was only just gone midday but the sky outside had darkened. Lauren turned on the lamp. No, fuck it, said Megan.

Lauren and Hannah listened to Megan's footsteps going down. Hannah pushed a strand of hair behind her ear. Somewhere, way down the hill, they heard a branch or tree falling in the bush.

What was it about Jackie? asked Hannah. Lauren thought about it for a bit. Let's just say she's been going through some mid-life issues—but she's seeing someone now. She threw a cast-iron griddle, she said, and tried to stab him. Hannah waited. Lauren set one eyebrow higher than the other, played with her ring, continued. I mean, sure I feel sorry for her and all that, and her brother, and the whole fucking crazy family, I'm sorry to see Tilly on the receiving end, but at the same time, I've got to tell you, I am perfectly happy with her not turning up last night. You can't have a conversation with her any more, a normal female conversation; she's changed, the change has changed her. And the job, Lauren continued, lifting her arms and clacking her bangles, that's changed her too. She walked into it, no experience, and bam, she's promoted twice in one year. It's counterproductive, isn't it—well, that's what I think—going into a job you know nothing about then being given all that responsibility? But she's always been a good talker, Jackie, God bless her heart and soul, and I'm sure that's a prerequisite for that kind of job, crapping on. But there's got to be something more, hasn't there? People tell her she's the best and she starts to believe it. Then your husband wins a seat in state parliament, he's in the papers, he's out doing things, important things, and you probably start to feel a bit inferior, don't you? You get paranoid. Maybe even a bit competitive. You want to prove you're on top. But it's events promotion! said Lauren. She brings out arena ballet shows, Chinese acrobats, prancing horses.

She got up and stoked the fire.

Did she get him? asked Hannah. Lauren turned to look at her: tall, lithe, upright, head turned like a bird's. With the knife, said Hannah: did she get him with the knife? No, said Lauren. She put a log on and closed the door.

Is it afternoon yet? Lauren was looking at the two empty glasses on the table under the lamp and the half-full wine bottle beside them. She picked the bottle up and poured them both a drink.

So what actually happened? asked Hannah. The devil got inside her, said Lauren, deadpan, and she turned into a witch. Marshall tried to get that devil out but when he couldn't, and the devil started spitting and snarling, he retreated into his work. The devil took over, made Jackie bleed rivers, then he stopped up her womb, shrivelled her breasts, hunched her back, made her hair lank, turned her fingernails to claws. Gave her breath the smell of rotten meat. Put a wart on her nose, a knife in her hand. A mad fury in her eye. Greer, said Lauren, uninterrupted, says the woman who lashes out in menopause has found 'the breach in her self-discipline' that leads ultimately to her freedom. She can be mad, if she wants; she can be anything. She's not made of sex any more, she's declaring her liberty from it. But the guy doesn't get it, does he? His eye starts roving, looking for the pert ones still slave to the only effective weapon they ever had. And no, don't look at me like that, said Lauren, turning; you lose that weapon, Hannah my darling, and you've got to find another. But they're all inferior, aren't they? Brain. Bravado. Old-fashioned self-belief. That's why we want a man to hug and not fuck us, isn't it? We're storing up the idea of the hug for later, so when he doesn't want to fuck us any more, when he wants to fuck everything *but* us, we've still got something to fall back on.

She drank. Fuck, I hate getting old. Hannah looked

down at her breasts. At least you've got both, said Lauren. Hannah looked up. Lauren raised an eyebrow, gulped her wine. It's the kids, she said, clacking her bangles again; we give them everything, they suck it all out of us. That's why we have to love them so much.

They both sat listening to the rain; each, secretly, in their own way, wishing the men would get back soon. Is Oliver okay? asked Hannah. The same, said Lauren. She pulled at her top, adjusted her neck, brushed something from her sleeve. He's living out of home now, she said, but I think he's off the stuff. Hannah nodded, and took an elegant sip. A friend of my sister's, she said, her son was caught dealing—it was after she and her husband had separated. The husband was having an affair with a woman in Sydney. Fay's friend went through his phone and found the texts. Apparently their marriage was looking shaky, anyway, and they were sleeping in different rooms and all that. But, well, this kid went off the rails.

It's the hotel, said Lauren; they can't help themselves.

They heard a car, or what sounded like a car, revving somewhere on the hill. Megan's Sam has just graduated though, hasn't he? said Hannah, brightly. Yes, said Lauren. Again Hannah pushed a strand of hair behind her ear. How did you meet Adam? she asked. Meet him? said Lauren. Oh, I don't know. We shared a couple of tutes, did that play Leon mentioned. Lauren looked into her glass, unsure whether to go on. At first I thought he was strange. He *was* strange—but then I kind of felt sorry for him. Then I fell in love with him. I guess he fell in love with me. Then—well. I haven't seen him in court for years—he used to do criminal stuff, now it's all corporate—but they say he's still the master of the put-down. That's the trick, isn't it? To make a virtue of your flaws? All that show, but something's broken. Everything I do, in my advocacy work, it's all driven by ego. I know that. Client satisfaction, it's a by-product: it's all about the performance. She raised one arm, let the bangles fall. But the kids keep you grounded, they knock you down to size: if anything's going to dampen a rampant ego it's a screaming, shit-smearing brat. That's why they gave us the coping mechanism, isn't it? So we cope. And the next thing you know you're forty-seven, with a sagging arse and a single tit. She laughed, throwing her head so far back that Hannah could see the roof of her mouth.

He must have been handsome though, said Hannah, when he was a student. I mean, he's still handsome now. That's true, said Lauren—but then she seemed to lose interest. She looked out to where the wind was shaking the trees. She was thinking about something, then the thought changed again. Keep your eyes off, she said, without turning around. She gulped her wine, smiled. Anyway, she said, jauntily, I better have a look at that soup.

It was all quiet down there; Megan knocked and waited.

Honey? Can I come in?

Tilly pulled the door back. She was wearing blue pyjamas with a grey hoodie over the top. She had a pale face, half-obscured, and long, straight, dyed-black hair. Is it okay if we have a little chat? asked Megan, aware that she'd already pushed her voice up too high. She lowered it again. Your dad and the boys have gone down the shops—why don't you let me in so we can have a little talk? Tilly seemed to be looking at the floor behind; she let the door go and gestured for Megan to come in.

It was the kids' room, where the various broods had come and gone over the years while the adults went about their business upstairs. There were three bunk beds, one on each wall, a cupboard next to the window and a dresser beneath it. On top of the dresser was a stack of picture books and teenage novels and a tennis racquet with a single ball resting on the strings. The window was closed, the blind drawn—it would otherwise have looked out onto the bush.

The first thing Megan noticed once her eyes had adjusted was Tilly's travel bag open on the floor near the cupboard with all the clothes spilling out. (And yet, she thought, she still hasn't got out of her pyjamas.) Next, the blue bucket on the floor near the furthest bunk with a small quantity of dirty water in it. Then the drip gathering on the ceiling above. Last, aside from the slight swampy smell coming off the bucket, was that fusty teenage odour, familiar from her own kids, close and cloying.

Tilly was sitting cross-legged on the bottom bunk near

the window, a stack of pillows between her and the wall. Her phone was on the bedcover, screen down. You could hear the rainwater churning in the pipes.

I only want to see if you're okay, said Megan. You did that before, said Tilly. They held each other's gaze; Tilly looked away. She picked up her phone with a languid hand and slid her thumb across the screen. Megan took a chair from the corner and placed it in the centre of the room.

It was not a kids' room any more but a teenage room which already in the short time they'd been there looked like any other teenage room you'd find anywhere in the world: the half-eaten plate of breakfast, the pair of knickers hanging off the cupboard door, the strewn clothes, the unmade bed. The smell. You people have no idea, Tilly was saying; I don't care if Uncle Rylan jumped from a rooftop café and killed himself. What do I care about that? Who's ever going to miss Uncle Rylan? There was an electric charge coming off her. What did he ever do? What did any of you ever?

But your father's trying, said Megan. The phone rang, buzzing and bouncing manically on the bed. Tilly picked it up. There was a tinny voice at the other end. Megan tried not to hear. She remembered Leon, at the same age, and the fire he had in his belly. *I'm going to tell the stories people don't want to hear*, he'd said, *that's how we'll change the world.* But by forty he was an alcoholic and his second marriage was fried. An old boss—what was his name?—gave him a fortnightly opinion piece but they buried it in the supplements. Say what you like, Lee—but no-one was listening.

Anyway, said Tilly. Megan had all this time been staring at the damp spot above the bucket where a new drip, a half-drip, was forming. I don't know, said Tilly, putting her phone facedown, if there's much point us talking any more. She seemed suddenly to have grown to twice her age. I appreciate your concern, Megan, really I do; I know you're a good person. There was a quiver in her eyes. Mum and I are no good. Dad too. She looked up and blinked. What a beautiful girl, thought Megan. I don't really know what else to say, said Tilly, the hood half-covering her face, eyes glistening, jet-black hair hanging down. I don't really want to talk. You only get one life. A while ago at school this story went around, I still don't know if it's true, about this girl, my age, whose parents had split up. (But I thought you didn't want to talk, thought Megan.) The father was living in Darwin and he offered to pay for her to come up and see him. She didn't want to go but her mother said she should. She was tall, long legs, thin ankles; her dad got her a seat by the exit door so she could stretch out. Halfway to Darwin, over the desert, the door blew off and the girl was sucked out. There was nothing anyone could do. The other passengers managed to hang on to their seats and the plane limped into Darwin. It was the middle of the day, a bright-blue sky, and this long-legged girl went floating down through the air. It was way out—way, way out. No-one saw her fall. Why would anyone be looking up, to see a thing like that? She was out there two weeks before they found her. Animals had eaten her face. She didn't want to go. She said to her mum she didn't want to go. Her long legs put her in that seat. What did she live for? What was the point?

So, you see, said Tilly, turning again and locking eyes: *I am not going to be that girl.*

Fuck me, said Evan, that's heavy.

The rain had carved channels out of the dirt on either side of the driveway, fanning out into muddy deltas across the road below. Marshall and Evan were in the front, Adam and Leon in the back. They'd made a dash with two umbrellas. It felt weird being in the car that Tilly had slept in; they could still smell her, faintly, perfume, shampoo, and something else like skin and hair and pores.

All right boys, said Evan, party time! No-one responded. Jesus, he said, it's like a fucking funeral in here. Marsh? Come on. You were all fired up when you got here and now it's all misery-me. Marshall put the car in reverse and turned around to look. Fuck, Evan, he said, for chrissakes, can't you see? I shouldn't have come, there'll be shit when I get home; my daughter won't speak to me, she's spent the night in the car; this is all fucked up, mate, totally fucked up. All the time he was saying this he was reversing the car down the driveway through the rain. Adam and Leon didn't know where to look, they glanced at the side of Marshall's face then behind them to see how he was going.

And you know what's happening back there, don't you? he said. I mean, Megan's a great woman and all that but, I'm sorry, she's also a fucking interfering bitch. She'll be down there now, for sure, the others too, giving Tilly the third degree. What happened, love? Are you all right? Have you heard from Mum? Is she all right? Can I use your phone? Just for a sec? They're not doing *that* are they? said Adam. Jesus you're a bunch of knuckleheads, said Marshall: do you really think they haven't already schmoozed up to Tilly, used her phone, spoken to Jackie, stabbed a couple more knives in my back? Oh come on, Marsh, that's a bit rich, said Leon: they're our wives and partners, mate, they're not a pack of fuckin' hyenas. Yeah, well, that's a matter of opinion, said Marshall, and he put the car in drive.

They were out on the road now; Marshall turned the wipers up high. I think you might be making a big deal out of this, said Evan, I don't think it's all that bad. Sometimes, you know, women just give me the shits, said Marshall. Do you know what I'm saying? I mean, if they want to take over the world, just fuckin' take over the world, stop fuckin' cheering and jeering from the sides. Do you know what I mean? Life's complicated, you think we don't know that? But we're trying, for fuck's sake, aren't we? I don't think Evan's saying you're not trying, said Adam. Shut your fuckin' mouth will you, Adam, you fuckin' know-it-all, said Marshall. Honestly, mate, I just won a fuckin' seat in state parliament, I'm representing my constituents—so tell me, where's the love been coming from for you lately? Evan turned and gave Adam an ironic sort of *oo-take-that* look. Honestly, guys, I love you all, you know, said Marshall, but things are shit for me at home right now; a bit of understanding wouldn't go astray.

Marshall decided to concentrate on the road. He was driving slowly, but the rain was coming down so hard that the wipers could barely keep up. The car came around a corner, then down a short, straight run, then started descending more sharply around a long, sweeping bend. Evan was fiddling with the radio, looking for the football, but all he could find was static. The unfinished conversation hung there. But they were all so conscious of the rain now and the stupidity of going out in it to get a loaf of bread and a couple of bottles of wine that no-one said anything. They looked out through the arcs the wipers made and tried to see what was ahead. Marshall negotiated the bend, in places the water was gushing over the road, and they were just coming to the end of it when he braked.

Fuck! said Evan. What's that? said Leon. Shit, said Marshall. The hill above had slipped. A big swathe of earth had come down over the road, blocking their way and going on to carve a tract through the bush below. On the mound in front a stand of acacia bushes still stood, rooted, upright, as if nothing had happened.

Shit, said Marshall, again. What do we do? said Evan. Can you get around? said Leon. Give us an umbrella, said Evan. Leon and Evan both threw open their doors and put up their umbrellas. The rain sounded like a waterfall, roaring in. Put your lights on high! shouted Evan. Marshall flicked them up. Pyooew, said Adam. He and Marshall watched Evan and Leon moving first to one side, then the other, trying to figure out how even Marshall's four-wheel drive Mercedes could ever get over or around.

Sorry about before, said Marshall, out of nowhere; I've got a lot going on, but I shouldn't have snapped. That's okay, said Adam. They had nothing else to say; with the mound of earth and bush in front of them and the rain pelting on the roof, everything else seemed petty. The other two got back in the car, bringing in the smell of dirt and rain.

It's blocked, said Leon; we're going to have to turn around. How the fuck am I going to do that? said Marshall. You'll need to back up, said Leon; there's a driveway about half a k back. Marshall lifted his hands off the wheel and turned his palms up as if to say *and*? Put your hazards on, said Evan. Again there was the rush of rain as the doors opened and again Evan and Leon threw up their umbrellas.

It was a tricky manoeuvre all right, but after a while Marshall got the hang of it, his head turned, one arm wrapped around the headrest on the passenger side. Adam knelt up on the back seat and pushed himself into the corner so Marshall could see: Yeah, that's good, to the left, steady, straight. The back wipers were cleaning the window in quick, manic strokes while the hazard lights lit the comical figures on the road above; Evan waving one hand out from under his umbrella and Leon, further up, shouting: Yep, all good, no dramas, you're good.

A voice, barely discernible, emerged from the radio-crackle and then was lost again. It felt quiet and calm in the car, all the craziness was outside. Marshall was in the zone, looking back, taking instructions, moving the wheel this way then that, almost without thinking. When he spoke, it sounded as if the words had come out of a dream.

My life's fucked, said Marshall. Adam had to look around and study his face to be sure he was talking to him. Marshall didn't make eye contact. It's hard to pin down when it all went wrong, he said, but I think I can guess. You're smart, mate, you're a lawyer, you know what it's like to get caught in lies. I lived truly once, he said, back in the days when I was a student, in student politics and that: do you remember? Back then those two things, living and truth, just sort of went hand in glove. And we were tolerant, too, weren't we? We forgave people. That's probably the other thing that happens when you live the truth, you find it easier to forgive. Jesus said that, or something like that, didn't he? I've got so much shit going down in my life at the moment, Adam, said Marshall, I couldn't even start.

Adam was looking at the side of Marshall's face but he

wasn't really listening. With Leon's story still fresh in his mind all he could think of was that dreadful student production and that scene after the fire with them all sitting around and Marshall as Tuzenbakh saying: *And what a vision I had then of a happy life! Where has it gone?*

Marshall braked. Evan and Leon were waving their arms around; Evan for Marshall to stop, Leon to point like a traffic cop at what they now realised was a steep gravel drive. They were encouraging Marshall to back in, so he could turn the car around.

Yeah, well, he said.

He began to reverse up. As soon as he got the rear in, the nose poking out onto the road, the front and back doors opened, the sound of rain rushed in, and Evan and Leon dived in after.

Jesus! said Evan. They both shook their umbrellas and folded them down and pulled the doors closed. Phew, said Leon. We should tell someone, said Adam. But they had no phone and for a moment there was only the sound of the radio static and the rain.

They headed back up the hill. If we see a car, or a light on, said Adam, let's stop. They all thought this was a good idea but the trouble was they saw neither. When they finally saw their own driveway and the light on high up in the living room it felt like they'd stumbled onto civilisation deep in the heart of darkness.

The four men trooped in downstairs: Evan first, then Adam, then Leon. Marshall was at the rear. The door to Tilly's room was closed. First shower, said Evan. Second, said Leon. Evan called out—Hey! The road's blocked!—but everything upstairs was quiet.

What are you doing? said Lauren, coming out of the kitchen. The road's blocked, said Evan, with a little lift of his shoulders. Hannah was in the living room. The road's blocked, said Leon, to her. What's going on? said Megan, from below— there was no hiding it, she'd just come out of Tilly's room. I'm having a shower, said Evan. It's a landslide, said Leon. We'll use the white bread, said Lauren, and she went back to the kitchen. Is she okay? asked Marshall, looking down. Megan nodded, but didn't speak. Marshall stood in the living room and put his back to the fire. Hannah looked out the window. Is there a bucket? said Evan. He was standing at the head of the hallway, pointing behind.

The roof was leaking onto the carpet directly above Tilly's room. Everyone started looking for a bucket. Megan came back from the kitchen with a big pasta pot and positioned it below the leak. They all stood, looking up. Bloody hell, said Leon. It's the leaves, said Marshall. The water dripped, loud and tinny at first, then with a *pweup*, into the pot.

They made a roster. When the egg timer went off you had to set a small saucepan temporarily under the leak, empty the pasta pot in the bath, take the saucepan away, put the pot back, re-set the timer and put a tick beside your name on the list. That took a while. Evan had his shower. Leon had one after—and Hannah went in with him. Lauren noted it, and went back to her soup.

Adam started microwaving the frozen slices of white bread. What were you talking about before? he said. Marshall should go home, said Lauren, and take Tilly with him. She kept stirring the soup. But the road's blocked, said Adam. Yes I know the fucking road's blocked, Adam, you just told me that, said Lauren, spitting the words out under her breath; I'm telling you what we were talking about *before* you came back and told us the road was blocked. If we knew the road was blocked, Adam, dick, there'd be no point in saying they should go home.

Have you been drinking? he said. Get the bowls, she said. He got seven bowls from the cupboard. Eight, she said. He got another. Ah that's better, said Evan, coming in freshly showered. Where's Meg?

She was on the couch in the corner of the living room with Marshall, talking. Marshall was holding one side of his head like it hurt. Megan was leaning in close to catch his eye. When Adam came in from the kitchen carrying the basket of microwaved bread he could see how she even had a hand on his knee. Evan followed with two bowls of soup.

Soup's up! he said. Leon and Hannah entered, separately,

from their room. Hannah's hair was wet. Oo hello! said Evan. Shut up, said Hannah. What's going on over there? said Leon. There was an awkward silence then while all five—Lauren had come in from the kitchen too, carrying more soup—stared into the living room at Megan and Marshall together on the couch.

The egg timer went off. They looked at the roster. Evan emptied the pot while the others sat down to lunch. Megan took a tray down to Tilly. When she came back Marshall thought it best to tell everyone what they'd been talking about. We're all friends here, he said. Megan took most of the conversation. She said how tricky it was with kids at that age and how we all know you can't always indulge them, but, by the same token, they'd agreed that maybe in this instance Marshall had been a little insensitive about the extent of the emotional impact of his brother-in-law's suicide and how, in a father's book, coming here might have seemed like a good idea while in truth maybe Tilly should have stayed at home. Marshall nodded at that. He looked tired.

Megan's right, he said, this father–daughter thing is tough. But it was going to be fireworks back there. We'll get in the car and get away from this, I thought, that's the best thing to do. But maybe I misread it; maybe I made a mistake. We all make mistakes, mate, said Evan, sitting down. I've had a lot going on, said Marshall, with the new job, I know I've neglected her. And maybe she hasn't agreed with all the decisions I've made. I know she's got involved with all this political stuff—occupy and anarchy and all that—but in the end you've got to follow your conscience, don't you? I mean, I didn't make the party's policy but, all the same, I'm not going to go howling in the streets in protest about it either. You've got to work within the system. You can't change major political decisions just because you think you might upset your teenage daughter.

Of course not, said Megan, and no-one would expect you to, but you've got to keep your antenna up, too, be sensitive to how they see things. They're the only thing we might have, said Adam, to prove we were even here. It's true, said Hannah, who had been quiet all this time (they all looked up at once), you complain about your children but don't forget they'll be a comfort to you in your old age. You, Megan, now Sam's graduated, do you think he's going to let you live on the street? The best superannuation you can have, said Leon, is a kid with a career. They all laughed.

It's true, said Evan, I'm a bit younger than you guys, but what's it going to be like for us once those fully qualified baby boomers start clogging up the system? Doesn't matter how many kids you've got. You're fucked, aren't you?

A strange new society is apparently erupting in our midst, said Adam. He looked up from his soup. It's from that book in the toilet, he said. The earth can't sustain itself, said Hannah, it's either adapt or die. It's going to get ugly for sure, said Leon. We've got to change our ways. Evan flapped his hands: *The sky is falling! The sky is falling!*

Tilly appeared at the top of the stairs.

Everything seemed to stop. Even the rain falling into the gutters and leaking into the stainless steel pasta pot with a steady *drip-drip-drip*—even this seemed to stop.

She'd changed out of her pyjamas and was dressed in black jeans and a black top, her hair looped behind one ear. She was carrying her empty bowl and plate. No-one knew what to say. Most of them hadn't seen her up close like this since at least the start of the year. She'd filled out: her breasts, her cheeks, her hips. Her skin was dotted with ruby-red pimples, she still had some dark eyeliner clinging to her lashes and lids. Megan took the things from her and balanced the spoon back in the bowl.

Thanks, said Tilly—but not to Megan. I appreciate your concern, everyone, really I do. But I'm okay. I'm happy to go back tomorrow, Dad, with you. She held her father's gaze. He looked down, and across. Tilly turned and walked back down the stairs. They heard the door below click.

She's a lovely girl, isn't she? said Hannah. She is, said Lauren. I know she's going through a phase, but what other kid would do that, say that? Everyone nodded. Adam and Leon, then Lauren and Hannah, began relaying the dishes to the kitchen. They kept going on about it, each in their own way, what a sweet girl Tilly was and how lucky Marshall was to have her. He said nothing, did nothing. The table was cleared around him.

All right folks, said Evan. Scrabble, cryptic crossword, Monopoly, strip poker? Story time? He opened the door of the wood heater and stuffed a couple more logs in. Well?

I've got one, said Megan.

It was just after three; there were two bottles left. They agreed to wait before they opened the first. A pot of tea was made, and the tray set on the low table.

I thought about this before, said Megan, when we were talking about getting old. I didn't think it was a story but now after listening to the others I guess it is. Anyway, I haven't been able to think up another.

I personally think it's one of the big issues of our time. (She was prefacing the work a little more seriously than had seemed necessary till now.) I mean, we can't ignore the fact that the hospital system is in chaos, under-funded, crisis-ridden, while millions of us are preparing to book ourselves in. Anyway, said Megan, I got this story from the horse's mouth, so to speak, last year when I was on my way up to the Territory. I drove up, in a hire car—Evan, you know all this—so I could take a few shots along the way: Flinders Ranges, Lake Eyre, the Centre. I'd hired it for a month. I was going to take it at a leisurely pace to Alice, spend two weeks out at Yuendumu, then drop the car back at Alice and fly home. Everything was going nicely, I'd spent two nights at Eyre (I've got to show you guys the photos some time, it was stunning) and was on the road from there to Oodnadatta when in the middle of nowhere, out of mobile range, the car blew up. I say the middle of nowhere, but in fact I wasn't waiting long by the side of the road with the bonnet up when a car appeared in the distance.

So anyway, said Megan, as I say, this car pulls up—late model, green, I'm not good with cars—driven by a woman about my age who said she was going the same way. Her name was Abbie. I told her what had happened and we decided it would be best to leave my car there and ring the hire company when we got to Oodnadatta where we reckoned there'd be mobile reception for sure. I put a note under the wiper with my number at the bottom. I got my stuff, put it in Abbie's car and off we went.

Lesbian sex in the desert, said Evan.

Abbie was a nurse, said Megan, giving Evan neither oxygen for his first joke nor the time to tell a second, and as it turned out she was on her way from Melbourne to the remote community of Lajamanu, west of Tennant Creek, to work in the health clinic there. I can take you most of the way, she said. Why don't you cancel the hire car when we get into town, get a refund then come with me as far as Alice and bum a lift to Yuendumu? It sounded like a good idea; I'd save myself a couple of thousand dollars and avoid having to do the whole thing on my own. They're long roads out there, and nothing much to see.

Megan picked the story stick up off the table.

It didn't take long to get talking, she said—Surprise, surprise, said Evan—and I told her about what I did and how I was heading out there to follow up on that doco and exhibition I did about the first anniversary of *Sorry*, to see what things were really like all these years later. Get the local folk to talk to camera, tell their stories, shoot it straight.

Anyway, we kept talking. Abbie tells me she's single, has been a nurse all her working life and is heading out to Lajamanu to make a new start because of all the crap going down in the hospital where she used to work. She was a big woman, with a plain face and a big brown mole on her cheek; her hair was short, less than a crew cut, like it had been shaved. She saw me looking at it. A long story, she said. Then she stared out the windscreen, like the story unravelling in her mind was as long as the road ahead. Well, I said, pointing. Abbie laughed. Yeah, all right, she said.

Megan: Waiting Lists...

I don't know if you know, Megan, said Abbie, how hospitals work—or don't work, as the case may be—but sadly these days they're not much more than get well factories. Sick people

133

come in, we fix 'em up as quickly and cheaply as we can, and out they go again. There's not much time for any of that Florence Nightingale stuff. *Key Performance Indicators*, that's the mantra: people are numbers, even sick people. Especially sick people. It's an obsession. I don't know when it started—it's already lost in the mists of time—but someone at some point decided that the way to improve a screwed-up health system was to ask the bean counters to make it more 'efficient'.

It became a numbers game. The government put a carrot in front and a stick behind: move the patients through faster and you'll be rewarded, slower and you'll be punished. And you see, Megan, in my opinion, the way the modern human being is made, you're always going to be more focused on getting the reward than copping the punishment: people will take all kinds of crap, as long as there's a tax break, an interest-rate drop, a performance bonus. It's like the dog getting whipped and then given a little crunchy treat. Doesn't matter how much pain it's suffered, the master—*its master*—has given it a little crunchy treat. For free. Or so it thinks.

Abbie had an easy way of talking, a soft voice, like someone who's always had to move quietly through the corridors and rooms. She talked without looking at me, her eyes on the road, but her body language said she was getting ready to share something, that I wouldn't need to prompt her, ask questions or anything like that. And I was happy to listen.

Because, she was saying, as we know, nothing's for free in this world, there's always someone owed something. At the hospital where I worked, this exchange had been going on for years: you reduce your waiting lists and we'll give you commensurate funding. One patient off the list? *Ker-ching*. Two patients? *Ker-ching, ker-ching*. The more patients we get rid of, the more government money we'll get to make improvements to the system. There was only one catch: we *couldn't* reduce our waiting lists. For every branch you pruned off the top, two more roots would grow at the bottom. We had to move the patients through faster but, without more funding, how were we going to do that? A lot of us were working up to sixteen-hour shifts, getting rid of patients as fast as we could, but the place was still chronically underfunded. It felt like we were going to go around in this circle forever.

Then one evening, when things had finally gone quiet after a terrible day, we were standing around the nurses' station talking and someone said, sort of off-the-cuff: If only we had a few patients we could get rid of quickly, then we might start to get in front.

What if, for example, said Beckie—a lovely girl, enthusiastic, committed—we discharged ten patients tomorrow morning instead of two? When we submit our monthly figures that would mean a five-fold increase in our funding. But how do we do that? someone asked. Find some patients who aren't that sick, said someone else. Or, said another, who aren't sick at all. And how do we do that? I asked.

Listen, said Beckie, lowering her voice, I've been thinking. We make up *fake* patients, add them to the list—hip replacement, gall bladder, skin cancer, whatever—move them up as we normally would until they reach the top, then we treat them, report on them, and discharge them. I've spoken to Heather in admin, said Beckie, still whispering, and she says it's a walk in the park. We start with a few, so it doesn't look odd; just a bit more stress than usual. More diagnoses, more referrals. But we're nurses in the public health-care system, she said, smiling; we rise to the occasion, don't we? So, on top of the massive number of patients we're already moving through, we somehow manage to move these new ones through too. And then, when the numbers go up again, we miraculously step up and move them through as well. And for every patient, a payment. We'll play them at their game, ladies, because we know for them it *is* one. We'll treat more or less the same number of *real* patients, but we'll have more money to do it: we'll be able to give them more attention, better care, treat them like human beings, all the things we came into the profession for. A deceitful act, said Beckie, but done for the greater good.

Well, said Abbie, continued Megan, what could we say? It was a no-brainer. None of us had to look too deep into our consciences to agree that in this case the end justified the means. There were five of us at the nurses' station that evening, plus Heather upstairs: we all had the computer access and know-how we needed to pull it off. In fact, it was almost *too* easy. To the hospital bosses, patients had become so many figures in a column, a long way from the pissing, shitting, farting, sweating, bleeding, suppurating bodies we had to deal with every day. They were never going to know whether Jill Blow, for example, liver patient, really *had* been in Bed 12, 3 East. How were *they* ever going to know that?

Abbie turned and looked at me, said Megan, with a huge grin on her face, and in that moment I got some idea of the buzz those nurses must have felt when they huddled together talking that night.

So, Abbie continued, at first we just added a couple of phantom patients to the records. We gave Heather the details and she dropped them into the system. The 'patients' worked their way up the list, Heather let us know when their appointment times had been 'sent', then on the appointed day we 'admitted' them. They were elective surgeries mostly, simple stuff, in and out in a day or two. No-one knew they didn't exist.

We called ourselves the gang of six and we all had our areas of expertise and allotted tasks. The key early members were me, Beckie, her friend Ange, Heather, Lisa, who liaised with our contacts in Emergency so we could start taking patients from there, and Keely, who was doing an evening writing course and volunteered to create the patients for us, their names, backgrounds, medical histories and treatments.

Patrick Henshaw, male, 52, married, two children, history of gallstones, attacks more frequent and severe, admitted 2 North Monday 15 October, discharged Wednesday 17. The first week went well, a couple of voluntary patients in and out without incident, and on Friday we all went out to celebrate. The next week we increased the numbers slightly and, again, everything went smoothly. Our project was underway.

It's incredible, when you think about it, said Abbie, what five nurses and an administrative assistant in a public hospital could get away with. The following week, and the week after that, we increased the numbers again. It was too easy. Of course we weren't doing this for any selfish reasons, there was nothing in it for us personally, and ironically the extra funding in the first instance went straight into the pockets of the bosses upstairs through performance bonuses. But the side effect was that, in the eyes of the hospital, we were turning ourselves into saints and martyrs. Somehow, we were keeping on top of this spike in admissions and still giving the best patient care possible. Within the first few months of the first phantom patient being admitted we were, the records showed, handling an almost seven per cent increase in admissions overall, with no visible decline in patient care. An administration email went around congratulating the nursing staff on dealing with the extra workload with great professionalism in these, they said, 'trying times'. We printed this email out and stuck it up in the nurses' station and that Friday night at our usual gathering we drank the best champagne we could buy.

Then we ramped it up. By March last year we were pushing through anything up to seventy extra patients a week. It was like a well-oiled machine. The bean counters upstairs had no choice but to reward us—they were the ones who'd set the rules. At the beginning of the next month, on our ward alone, we were given a new ECG unit, a new defib, three new sphygs plus a whole bunch of new bibs and bobs we'd been requesting for over a year. That week there was a real bounce in our step as we went about our rounds.

But then things got complicated. The union was looking at the figures too. Here was hard evidence, they said, for the case we've been arguing for years about better pay and conditions. The system's in crisis, nurses are bearing the brunt. Staffing levels must be increased, workloads reduced, and pay rises awarded across the board. Fat chance, said the hospital administrators and the government, so the union started ratcheting things up.

Under any other circumstances this would have been a good thing—we were all members, it was a hard-working union and it deserved our respect—but the trouble was, all this agitation was putting the spotlight on our little 'project'. The administrators started asking questions. Our friends in Emergency were under the hammer enough without the auditors sniffing around: Lisa told us she wanted out. We replaced our phantom Emergency patients with phantom elective-surgery patients instead. These lists were slower—to be honest they moved like glaciers—but they were an easier place to bury our lies. Then the auditors started sniffing around our ward too.

We all met, I remember, at the pub that Friday, at our usual table in the corner up the back, to discuss the situation. Ange had got cold feet too. I was prepared to let her go—I was having second thoughts myself—but Beckie called her a coward and reminded her of what we'd already managed to do. But Ange wouldn't be moved. She said we needed to stop now while we could—we've proved our point, isn't that enough? But sometimes, said Beckie, you've got to stand up for what you believe in. And when you get caught? asked Ange. Caught for what? asked Beckie. What have we done wrong? Ange shook her head. By the time the meeting in the pub adjourned that night our gang of six was a gang of four.

Abbie pointed at a roadhouse in the distance. Are you hungry? she asked. She put her indicator on. I need to get petrol. There were three or four trucks in the carpark, and a couple more along the verge. We found a spot and went inside.

Well, said Abbie, once the chicken wraps and chips were on the table, where was I? Yes, the gang of four. I'm not boring you, am I? I shook my head—but I couldn't help thinking how different this trip would have been if I were still in my car, listening to my talking book, eating my trail mix, stopping when I felt like it to take shots.

Abbie took a big bite out of her wrap and stared chewing. Because, you know, she said, the funny thing is, telling it all to you, it sounds so stupid. Do you know what I mean? Six women coming up with this scheme, let alone having the balls to go through with it. Who does that kind of stuff any more? We felt like we had to stick it out—if we were smart there's no reason, we thought, why we couldn't keep adding phantom patients to the elective-lists for years. We'd jumped ahead too quickly, that was all, and needed to pull it back. Lisa and Ange were out of the group but we felt like we could trust them; nurses are loyal to their kind. But you should eat your lunch.

I took a bite and put it back on my plate. Abbie pushed the bucket of chips across. The woman behind the counter called to say our coffees were ready and Abbie got up to get them. I'm trying to remember everything, said Megan, all the detail. She sipped her tea. Pscht, that's cold, she said.

So, said Abbie, all the best-laid plans. When we started our shift together the following Monday the game had changed again. Our four ward doctors had been replaced—we'd seen none of these new ones before and it seemed as if they'd been selected to be as up themselves as possible—and an auditor was assigned to 'study our work practices'. He shadowed us for most of that afternoon and then appeared out of nowhere again on Tuesday. We played things carefully, dropped a few extra patients onto the lists but did nothing else to arouse suspicion. On Wednesday the auditor called a few of us into his office to ask questions; we handled them okay but things were getting hot, we knew it, and we needed a new strategy.

That Friday at the pub we started brainstorming ideas: we either had to come up with something new or close the project down. We went through a whole list of scenarios, but still hadn't come up with anything inspiring when Beckie, in her call-a-spade-a-spade sort of way, said: What we need are some *actual* patients, to put them off the scent. If we could have one or two *actual* people pop up in the beds we've assigned to phantom patients, just when the auditors come looking for them, they'll start to think that maybe these patients *are* real, the lists *are* growing and these nurses *are* working beyond the call of duty to clear them? Then, said Beckie, we might be able to get them off our backs and start bumping the numbers up again.

And that's when Keely mentioned the actors.

Keely was the one, said Abbie, continued Megan, taking the fresh cup of tea Lauren had poured, who was doing the writing course, remember? She'd met a girl there, Simone, whose boyfriend, Hayden, was an actor, and he'd been making some money on the side doing med-student patient simulations—stroke, pancreatic cancer, or whatever. He also did psychiatric stuff. He'd get a worksheet a couple of days beforehand with a list of symptoms to study and rehearse and a list of questions that the students might ask towards diagnosis. Then, on the day, for an hour and a half, sometimes two, Hayden would moan and groan, clutch his stomach, limp, whatever, and in role answer the questions the students then put to him. The pay's great, said Keely, better than hospitality. Hayden and a few of his actor friends had been doing it for a while.

If we could offer these guys a bit of money, she said, I see no reason why they couldn't play patients for us, at short notice if we needed, on the day for example when we had our ward inspections. We'd give them a name, age, background, ailment and a list of symptoms and ask them to swot up, then we'd 'admit' them and have them on display when the ward doctors or auditors came around.

But how do we pay them? I said. From the Christmas fund, said Beckie. What Christmas fund? said Keely. The Christmas Fund, said Beckie, that we get all the other guilty nurses to contribute to—the Christmas fund that will 'pay for dinner and drinks and a visit from Santa' at the end of the year. Keely, Heather and I took a while to catch on. We'll let the others who know what we're doing but who don't want to be involved ease their consciences by contributing: it's a small payment, we'll explain to them, for the benefits we're bringing to your wards. They won't disagree, trust me, said Beckie. To the Christmas Fund! she said, and we all raised our glasses.

It worked a treat. We gave Hayden cholelithiasis, gall-stones, a mild attack. We called him Callum Broadbent. We brought him in through the back door, doctored the records to show he'd come in the night before through Emergency, marked up his chart to say he'd been given morph on arrival and endone since and that he seemed to have settled down. We had him set up in bed watching telly when the ward doctor came through that morning around eleven. The doctor was in a hurry—they are always in a hurry. He checked the patient's chart, asked him a few questions, pulled the curtain around and lifted Callum's gown and pushed down here and there. Callum winced, as rehearsed, and said it was still a bit sore but nothing like last night when, he said, he'd been doubled over with pain and couldn't walk. The ward doctor said it seemed to have settled—he'd send him home that afternoon with pain-killers and instructions to go back to his GP in the next couple of days. If it flares up again, said the ward doctor, he may need to do something about it. The doctor left, and Keely, shadowing him, texted Beckie and me: *Gallstone patient all clear.* That afternoon we gave Hayden his payment and sent him on his way.

The next day, and each day after that for two weeks, we moved about half-a-dozen of these 'performance patients' through. We never gave them anything too complicated, an hour's preparation at most and nothing that was likely to get them rushed off to surgery. We'd email the actor their patient name, age, condition; they would do the performance and we would pay them thirty dollars an hour cash on discharge. Pretty soon we'd got our numbers back up to the same level as before but now we had *real* patients in our beds and doctors as eyewitnesses to it. It was going well. The auditors came back sniffing occasionally, like a dog who's left something behind, but we always had new patients ready to shut them up.

One day, an auditor came down to do the rounds accompanied by a bigwig supervisor woman with a lanyard and reading glasses on a chain. I had the great pleasure of showing them around one room in the ward where *every bed had an actor in it* and every performance was pitch perfect.

Well, said Abbie, standing up, I suppose we should get moving. We walked outside, the heat was like a wall, the car door handle burning to the touch. And it was funny, I remember, said Megan, when we got back in, there was a moment of hesitation: what was I doing with this woman, listening to this story? Because all the while I'd been listening, in the car, in the roadhouse, I was actually having more and more trouble believing it—I mean, it was far-fetched to begin with but now it just seemed crazy. Did all this really happen, I was thinking, actors playing patients in the public-hospital system to dupe money out of the authorities, or was it some kind of kooky fantasy of Abbie's that she was telling me to pass the time?

It's bullshit, said Marshall; no-one could pull off something like that, not with all the checks and balances in place nowadays. You think she was having me on? said Megan. They all shrugged. Tch, I knew it, she said, almost to herself.

It was still pouring. The pot bell went off. Leon got up to empty it.

All right, said Evan, fuck this. Anyone? Yeah, said Marshall. Yeah, said Hannah. Beside the fridge, said Lauren. Yeah, said Adam. Yeah, said Megan, all right. Half, said Lauren. Evan was bouncing up and down on the balls of his feet. And the San Pel, said Leon.

I can't believe all that was a lie, said Megan, falling back into the cushions. I so believed it when she started. It probably was true, said Adam, to some extent; they probably did add some phantom patients to the lists early on, but then she got caught up in the storytelling. We've all done that: does it matter? No, said Megan, I suppose not.

Ah! said Marshall, without sitting up from his slump, so when a politician tells a lie it's a hanging offence but when anyone else does it and says it's a story, that's fine! Yep, said Lauren, that's pretty much how it goes. It's a harmless lie, anyway, isn't it? said Hannah. But politicians' lies, Marshall, they can hurt people. Megan's hurt, said Marshall, look at her; her driving companion pulled her leg and now she's hurting. Megan gave him a wincing smile. Evan came back from the kitchen with two bottles of wine, a bottle of mineral water and seven glasses on a tray. Can you bring some cheese and crackers too? said Lauren. Jesus! said Evan. And take the empty cups back? said Megan. Jesus! said Evan, again. He's a good boy, isn't he? said Megan. He is, said Leon, grinning.

So, Adam, said Marshall, you're the lawyer: why do we think this Abbie woman was lying? We believed her at first, for a while, and then we didn't. Well, said Adam, I guess in the first place because we are hearing her story via Megan and as Megan became less convinced that the story was actually true, something in her demeanour started sending out signals to us. We began to read not the tale but the teller. Adam lined the glasses up and started pouring the wine. In law, he said, we have this ancient principle called 'legal fiction'. It basically means that something can be considered true even though it might not be. For example, a man, A, finds a bag of money in the woods; another man, B, comes along and says it's his and takes A to court to have what he says is his bag of money returned. I was riding through the woods on my piebald horse with the lame off-hind, says B, on my way to my sick brother's house to offer help to his poor wife and children and it must have fallen out of my saddlebag. The judge finds in his favour. There is no evidence, there are no witnesses. The judge just *believes*. Under the tenet of legal fiction, said Adam, a story no matter how unlikely can sometimes seem most true—and so will become, for legal purposes, *actually* true. Many anthropologists, he continued, believe we are the only animals capable of lying and that this is in many ways what distinguishes the human species and probably played a large part in our evolutionary success. So is it right to hold against us the very trait that separates us from the apes? Our ability to fib? We have Art, said Nietzsche, said Adam, so that we may not perish from the Truth.

He put the bottle down. Evan came back with the cheese and crackers: he had another bottle dangling from his fingers.

Where do you get all this shit from? said Marshall. How do you remember it all? I guess because it's worth remembering, said Adam. Evan put the things down. Not everything is worth remembering, said Adam, in fact, you could almost say that most of what people concern their heads with these days is not worth remembering at all and should be allowed to slip unnoted into history's abyss. But that's not the way it is, is it? He sipped his wine. Actually, most of us remember the stuff not worth remembering; the pointless, trivial stuff. But there's always a few swimming upstream, Marshall, trying to hang on to what might be useful.

Woo, said Evan, sitting down. Yeah, said Megan. I like listening to this, said Hannah. Go on, said Leon. Yeah, said Lauren. Well, said Adam, taking up a cracker and spreading it with King Island brie, I think we're living through interesting times, so far as truth is concerned. And one of the main reasons is that we have confused it with facts. Facts, to my mind, are as little to be trusted nowadays as lies, because there are so many of them. Call it data, if you like. But just because there are all these facts doesn't mean we should listen to them. In fact (ha!), when so-called truth comes at us in an avalanche like that, a thousand tiny bits, shouldn't we be more inclined to distrust it? Mightn't we be better off cutting through all the crap and like the judge in the case of the bag of money in the woods actually trust our instincts? Believe the unbelievable, even if—or because—it is a lie? Mightn't we be better off looking to get our truth these days through an artifice that truthfully says it is one?

Leon started clapping, a wry smile on his face. Art is going to save us, said Lauren, flatly. Maybe art can, said Adam, with a flourish of fingers, for the reasons I've just said. Reason, logic, science—they're exactly what got us into this mess in the first place.

That's a pretty sweeping statement, Adam, said Marshall, sitting up slightly, especially coming from a lawyer. That everything since Plato and Aristotle—reason, logic, law, government, civilisation—has been a waste of time and we ought to ditch it and start making up stories and plays and songs instead. When you put it like that, said Leon, actually, I'm with Ad. Me too, said Hannah, politics is fucked. It's a power trip, she said, it's got nothing to do with making the world a better place—sorry, Marshall, but it's not just me; ask half the world and I'm sure they'd agree. What Adam's saying,

149

she continued, a slight flush to her cheeks, is that the great enlightenment experiment has failed, reason has not saved us, and we're no closer than ever to understanding why we're here and what we should do, how we should get on, live with each other, communicate, share. All the systems we've put in place have failed. It's like that Japanese nuclear plant: *we have systems in place, it's all under control*—then along comes a giant wave. Global capitalism: *we have systems in place, the market can absorb the shocks*—and then. All that logic of systems starts to look pretty shaky, doesn't it? And all Adam's saying, I think— sorry Adam—is that in this kind of truth-poor environment maybe we need to look somewhere else to figure out how we should live?

Hannah was on the edge of the couch. Leon had a hand on the small of her back—it was hard to tell if he was holding her back or pushing her forward. Marshall, on the other hand, had slumped down again as if trying to protect himself from the blows. Well yes, said Adam, but I guess we should let Megan finish her story—I don't think she was asking for such a long answer to her question.

Phew, said Megan, shaking herself. So what *was* the question again?

They all laughed.

It had just gone five and an early winter evening was coming down. The sky was backlit, glowing. Evan looked out. I wonder how the Saints went? he said.

The rain was still coming in waves, slapping the roof, the windows, the walls. Everything strained and creaked. You could hear the legs of the table outside scraping across the deck and from everywhere a cacophony of gurgling, splashing, slurping. The sound of earth sucking water seemed to outdo even the mighty sounds of the sea.

So, said Megan. The roadhouse on the way to Oodnadatta. Abbie behind the wheel. What next? she said. Well, she continued, after the big success with all the actors in the ward that day, Keely, our go-between, dropped out. She said we'd got ourselves in too deep. So now it was just Beckie, Heather and me.

Well, the first result of this, said Abbie, was that the actors got cold feet too. The whispers went down the line, saying how Keely had bailed, and that sent a panic through them all. We rang around, tried to reassure them, offered more money, but they weren't interested. In fact, they thought we were crazy—and we probably were.

I'd wanted to be a nurse all my life, had sacrificed everything for it, and now here we were, just the three of us, taking all these risks, putting our careers on the line—and for what? A few extra dollars dropped into a broken system, money that should have been given to us without strings attached years ago. What we were doing had outrun our reasons for doing it, we were playing with patient lists now just because we could. But were we making any *difference*?

Then one day the nursing supervisor called the three of us into her office. She was a big woman, and that morning she seemed to have puffed herself up to twice her normal size. She started talking about the pressure we were all under, how we were all in the same boat, how stingy funding affected us all, not just the radical few; we are all fighting the same fight, she said, fiddling with her lanyard, and she would be the last to discourage suggestions from her staff about ways to improve efficiency. If one group of nurses is managing to clear their backlogs quicker than the others then she would be remiss in her duty—wouldn't she?—if she didn't enquire into their work practices to see if there might not be something there that she could adopt in other areas of the hospital. That's only natural, she said. But in doing this, you see, girls—she called us girls—in doing this enquiring, we have uncovered a couple of anomalies. It's understandable, of course, in a big public hospital, accommodating thousands of patients every week, that there might be a few record-keeping oversights. Maybe a patient has been wrongly assigned, maybe a patient has, according to the records, been discharged early, or late; sometimes we might even have patients on our records who don't seem to exist, or, at least, when we go looking for them, we can't find them.

Of course, said the supervisor, there may be a perfectly

reasonable explanation: the patient has been discharged and (unforgivably, I would have to say) the records have not been updated. Perhaps—I suppose this is possible—the patient has been transferred to another ward of the hospital and, again, surprisingly, the records have not been corrected. Or perhaps a really bad admission error has been made. John Smith, say, has been entered as Jim Smith, say, and when John Smith is subsequently found lying in a bed in 4 East and the record corrected, the non-existent patient, Jim Smith, has somehow—I don't know how—been left in the system? It seems far-fetched, true, that a professional nursing team could do that, but you never know. Or—let me speculate again—perhaps the patient whose name and details and medical history appear on our hospital records never existed at all? Now there's an idea. This one, for example, I wonder who she is?

The supervisor, said Abbie—hands on the wheel, glancing sideways at me—was holding up a sheet of paper so we could read it. Jacinta Rose, she said, female, thirty-two, severely infected cyst, upper right jaw, admitted yesterday am, operated on pm, moved post-op to Bed 9, 4 North late yesterday evening. But we can't find her. Anywhere. Shall we go up and have a look?

It all happened so quickly, the supervisor had barely finished the sentence before she was out of her chair, the sheet of paper rolled up and thrust in front of her like a pointing stick. We followed her into the corridor. She started making small talk—*It's a lovely day*—*Do you have weekend plans?—There's the new IV*—and we tried to stay on topic. *Yes, it is—No, not really—That must have cost a fortune.* But we knew we were going to the gallows.

When we got to the lift I excused myself, saying I'd left a patient for a urine sample in the toilet on my ward, and before the supervisor had a chance to object I headed for the stairwell. I came out on the fourth floor looking like I'd run a marathon and raced to the nurses' station where Ange, one of our original members, was on duty. Hurry, I said, the supervisor's coming, get me a gown, a bandage and a shaver or I'll tell her you're in on it too. Ange did what I said. In the toilets I stripped, hid my clothes in the sanitary bin, shaved half my head and flushed the hair down the toilet, wound the bandage around my jaw then ran to Bed 9, got in and 'fell asleep'.

The sheet had only just settled on me when I heard the *click-clack* of the supervisor's heels. Then I heard Beckie's voice. Yes, here she is, she was saying, it looks like she's sleeping; I think we've got her on morphine so it's probably best not to wake her. I heard the footsteps stop, then felt the shadow on the window side as the supervisor looked down at me. It was quite serious, Beckie was saying, and they had to remove some surrounding tissue; even her mother wouldn't recognise her when she came back from theatre. That was the last thing I heard before I felt the supervisor's fingers, pulling at the bandage.

So, said Abbie, that was that. We were dragged up before the hospital board, the others too, and asked to explain ourselves. There wasn't much to explain. The union backed us for a little while but then they saw the error of their ways. We'd brazenly manipulated the patient records of a well-known public hospital and we were going down. Forget about the public good, the means justifying the ends—there are systems in place to prevent that kind of thing.

Anyway, said Abbie, to cut a long story short, some time after this Ange told me she knew someone who worked in the remote communities up in the Territory. Apparently they're not so diligent with their record-keeping and there is no Board of Suits to tell you you're evil. You do what you can with the money you're given. That might suit me for a while. Abbie stared at the road ahead. Ah, she said, perfect timing. She was pointing at a road sign: *Oodnadatta 10*. So, she said, what's your story?

They all sat in silence for a while, thinking: *Oh, I see, now we're going to get another story, Megan's story within the story, and if that's the case then maybe we should look around for some more wine?* But then Megan, reading the room, said: No, that's it, that's the end. When we got to Oodnadatta I decided not to go all the way with her. The car rental company said they could get me a replacement the following day and would put me up for the night. And Abbie, she was weird—it *might* have been true, I don't know—but I wasn't sure I wanted to hear any more of her stories, or for that matter tell mine. She dropped me off. I said thanks and good luck. But I couldn't help looking at her crew cut as she drove away, thinking about the supervisor's expression and the plumber pulling the hair out of the toilet, the faces of the board when she got dragged up before them. I wonder if stories can change how things are in the world or if they're just us telling others what we think the world looks like? Do you know what I mean?

It was dark. Lauren pulled the curtains closed. Do you want to stoke the fire? she said. Evan did. Megan was still on the couch, thinking about her story and the question she'd asked at the end. Yes, said Adam, I think they do. Really? said Megan. Does me pointing a camera at a blackfella change anything?

Nothing changes anything, said Leon. They all looked at him. The power's elsewhere, he said, always has been—but no-one knows where elsewhere is. It might have been the politicians once, a long time ago. Writers and artists once had power to change things. People say it's business now, global corporations, the media, the new media—but I don't believe that either. They're powerless too, they're chasing an idea of power that even they know is elsewhere. People power? Nah. I don't believe it; no left-winger can believe it after what happened to Soviet Russia. Maybe that's power's natural property, said Leon, to coagulate, concentrate. Stalin. Mao. Pol Pot. Mugabe. The excitable energy and goodwill of the people, that great maelstrom of *peopleness*, all that fantastic fire is eventually distilled into one single despot. Maybe by its very nature power can't be a spread out thing. And that was the trouble, for someone like me, a journalist with a conscience: no-one changed anything unless he or she was lucky enough to be the one who became the despot, the right person in the right place at the right time in whom all that power was held. So no, Megan, or Adam, sorry, stories change *nothing*.

Megan was about to strike at her brother and his insidious idea, the way he'd turned her melancholy moment into his own smart brand of nihilism, but before she had a chance Marshall was talking. I've got a story, he said. Do you reckon I can tell it? Everyone looked at him. Shouldn't we eat? said Leon. Marshall threw his hands up. There you were, all hoeing into me, giving it to us politicians—we're liars, we don't do anything. Well, do you think I'm happy with the situation? (He was on his own trip again.) I mean, you talked about those people before, Leon—Lee?—in your story, the protesters, everyone shouting: *We want to change the world!* But what did they achieve? You try to make one happy, you put the other one's nose out of joint. We're too polite, we have to be. We've become polite-icians. And why? (No-one knew whether Marshall wanted an answer.) Because there are always two sides, he said. Never three. Or four. Or twelve and a half. It's always on the one hand this and on the other that. So how do you get hold of an issue that'll actually give you some traction? Politicians aren't leaders. Once were, not now. We're followers, folks. Real leaders are going to have to come from somewhere else. Sport maybe. I don't know. Guerrilla knitting. He drank. Anyway, he said, it's short, trust me—and I don't think it'll hurt anyone's feelings.

They all agreed that maybe they did have time for one more before dinner.

Well, said Marshall, putting his glass back on the table, this story is something another pollie told me just after I'd taken up my seat. It's about a Canberra backbencher and the problem he had with this guy in his electorate. Maybe stories don't change things—Megan, Leon—but things in the world *become* stories, don't they? It was yours, Megan, said Marshall, that made me think of it. It's about real estate, too, in a way, which should give a few people here a few laughs. It's called *Like Bartleby*. Contrary to the secret opinions of certain people in this room, I did pay attention at uni and if you remember in first year we studied Melville and he had a story about a clerk in an office who refuses to go home and actually ends up sleeping there and his boss, the guy telling the story, doesn't know what to do. Well this story is a bit like that, said Marshall, and he picked up the stick. That's why I've called it *Like Bartleby*.

Marshall: Like Bartleby…

The backbencher's name was Payley and his seat—unlike mine, which I wrestled from the blue bloods by a one per cent margin—was rusted on Labor, twenty per cent margin at the last election. Mostly outer suburbs with lots of new housing estates full of aspirational lower middle class which, as we know, is contemporary Labor's core constituency. All mortgaged to the hilt. They're popping up everywhere out there, these estates, like mushrooms after the rain. Fair enough. Why wouldn't the farmers want to sell? The land is worth jack shit as farmland but for housing it's worth millions. Most get sold off the plan: some newlyweds go out for a drive on a Sunday, turn off into one of the new streets that have been cut through the paddocks, have a look around and say: Yes, this block here, this looks nice. They visit the display suite, pick a house—the *Fortitude*, say, or the *Liberty*—and whack down their deposit. Six months later, they move in. It's a pretty efficient system, when you think about it, if anything it's been working a bit too well. But occasionally you get a spanner in the works.

Payley first got wind of it through his electorate officer; a reporter from the local rag had rung to say he was running a story and would his boss like to comment? The story was about a young Indian couple who had recently bought a house off the plan, they were expecting their first child and were pretty keen to move in. The woman was seven-and-a-half months pregnant. But the house was only a few weeks away from finished when someone started squatting in it. The couple had gone out there one Sunday for a look—there were still a few fittings to go in and some last-minute painting to be done—but when they put their faces to the window they saw a man sleeping on a mattress inside. They went to the display suite and spoke to the woman but she couldn't do anything and suggested they ring the police. The police came round and looked in through the window and banged on the door and then things started to get complicated. The couple said it was their house, yes, but naturally they weren't living in it yet, and no, they didn't have any documents with them to prove owner-ship. The cops banged on the door a few more times. Still the man inside didn't move. They suggested the couple take it up with the housing company—surely they were responsible for security while the house was being built?—and if they still had problems they should try the police again.

But after that it all went completely off the rails.

When the painters arrived the following Tuesday a small group was already gathered out the front of the house. They were all black. One of them, a well-dressed young woman, explained to the painters that she was a lawyer and that the house was off-limits because of a land-title claim currently underway; they would need to remove themselves from the site and check in with the developer: they would certainly not be doing any work here today. The painters left. The police arrived. The Aboriginal lawyer explained to them how the man inside was exercising his right to sit down in the land of his forebears and that the police would need to cast their judicial net a bit wider than mere 'trespass' if they wanted to stay involved. The police went away to confer.

About a week later, the electorate officer pulled Payley aside and told him what was going on and how the local paper was planning to run a story the following Monday. Payley cleared his social calendar and went out there on Saturday morning for a look.

Well, as you can imagine. There were about a dozen people now camped permanently in the front yard—still just dirt and building rubble with a portable toilet to one side. There was a hand-painted sign—*Always Was, Always Will Be*—strung along the fence and a black, red and yellow flag tied across the front window. Payley explained to them who he was, and how he was therefore the one probably best positioned to listen to their grievances. To that end, said Payley, he would like to talk to the gentleman inside. One of them got on their phone and made a call and told him to wait.

Payley stood on the footpath. He was wearing his suit and the day was already hot; the sky blue, the sun fierce, he could feel the sweat gathering under his arms. He let his eye roam over the landscape that made up, let's be honest, a big part of his electorate, and he wasn't sure he liked what he saw: scrappy paddocks with new houses going up in them, bulldozers parked in front of mounds of dirt, shiny cars cruising the streets and circling the courts and gathering at the display suite back there at the roundabout. My country, he thought. The protesters in the front yard were all watching him, quietly, with vacant stares—someone somewhere had a radio on, previewing the football. Then he saw a flash-looking red hatchback coming down the street.

It was the Aboriginal lawyer, dressed in a sharp skirt and jacket and knee-length black leather boots. Payley told the lawyer who he was but this didn't seem to impress her. She explained the situation and the legal precedents on which it was based. The old man inside—she kept calling him 'Uncle'— was exercising his basic human rights and until these rights were tested in an international court of law she was not sure what Payley, as a local member, could do. He tried to explain to her how parliamentary democracy worked, how the couple who had bought the house in good faith from the developer were as much entitled to a sympathetic ear as her so-called uncle, and as their duly elected local member he was that ear. It is always better to avoid the courts if we can, he said, and he explained how as a Labor man he was certainly alert to her cause and the deeper issues underpinning it but that he also believed in the power of honest conversation. I should at least, he said, have the opportunity to hear your uncle state his case.

By now the Saturday house shoppers were beginning to cruise the streets of the estate: whitebread Aussies, Chinese, Indians, Africans, Middle Easterns, all slowing down or stopping to look. The lawyer led Payley to the front door and opened it. He expected it to be cool inside but it was in fact hot and stuffy, with the air an oppressive mixture of cooked food, fresh paint, plaster, plastic and human breath. The air conditioner wasn't connected. All right, she said, he's in the lounge room, and she went back outside.

Payley could hear the radio in the front yard and muffled voices coming from somewhere inside the house. He passed a room in which people sat cross-legged in a circle playing some kind of board game: a few of them looked up. He walked further down the hall, past another room, this one with kids lying on their backs on mattresses with their game-screens held right up to their faces, then past the kitchen with something simmering on the stove. It was an open-plan house with a big living area out the back and a small paved courtyard that stopped abruptly at a treated pine fence. The living room was bare except for a double mattress and blanket in one corner. It was on this mattress that Bartleby was sitting.

He would have been in his seventies, at least, with a mop of white hair and a long white beard, his hands arthritic claws, the lines on his face carved as if out of black stone. He was blind, or almost; when Payley entered the room he could see Bartleby turn his head and look vaguely in his direction but his eyes never focused properly on him. They had a milky sheen. Payley hung in the doorway until he was sure the old man was at least aware of his presence and wouldn't be scared by his voice. He introduced himself as the recently elected local member of parliament. I've come for a visit, he said, to see what's going on—there are all sorts of rumours, as you can imagine. Bartleby was still looking through Payley. He didn't speak. Can I sit? asked Payley. He took his silence as a yes and sat cross-legged opposite—he'd never discussed things with a blackfella before but he figured that's what you do.

So anyway, said Marshall, going on, there they were: Payley the backbencher in his suit, Bartleby the blackfella in his old track pants and hoodie. Payley started by saying that, basically, there was a problem. A young couple had paid a lot of money to live in this house, hard-earned money, he said, money that doesn't come easy these days, and clearly they were upset that a group of people who had paid *no money*—no money at all—were now living in it instead. You see how this might seem unfair? Bartleby didn't answer. It is the dream of every young couple to own their own home, said Payley, to make a nest—the woman is expecting a baby—and you can see just by looking around at this estate here which is almost entirely pre-sold how many young couples are looking to make a nest and how many houses and estates we'll need to satisfy them. We can't just let anyone in to take these houses, they're not here for the taking, they're a reward for hard work and frugality.

Bartleby had his head cocked to one side, as if one ear heard better than the other. Payley left a decent pause; Bartleby filled it.

Now I've sat down, he said, I won't be getting up.

That was it—and even these few words sounded like they had struggled to get out. His voice wavered, his lips barely moved. (That's what made me think of the Bartleby story, said Marshall, and how this guy was him.)

Yes, said Payley, I understand how you've sat down, but you see my problem? We can't all just sit down where we want when we want, that would mean anarchy. Some places you can sit down, some you can't; a public place, you can sit down there, most of the time, with some exceptions, but a private place, you can't sit down there without permission. Do you understand? Payley was treating him like a child because he was acting like one. To get permission to sit down here, he said, you would need to go through a whole lot of processes— I won't go through them with you, they would make your head spin—with the purpose basically of getting permission to sit down from the person who bought and therefore *owns* the property you want to sit down in. That's what ownership means.

It was only then he realised some of the others in the house had gathered in the hallway at the far end of the living room to listen: young kids, a couple of young women, a middle-aged man. (The middle-aged man was the only one, thought Payley, who looked properly black, the others looked more or less white to his eyes—the kid with his face poking out from behind the middle-aged man's leg for all intents and purposes *was* white.) I am explaining to Uncle here, he said, turning, about ownership, how someone has already bought this house and to sit here like this, like Uncle is doing, is unfortunately against the law. At last one of the women spoke. She had broad hips and a wild head of hair. Uncle, she said, are you all right? This fulla's the one who doesn't belong here, not you, she said. Payley could see he was up against it, so he tried another tack. Come in, he said to the woman, come and join us, I have nothing to hide. On the radio out the front, very faintly, he could hear the sound of the siren to start the first quarter of the football and the distant roar of the crowd.

The group in the hallway all trooped in and lined themselves up behind Bartleby along the glass wall that looked onto the courtyard. Payley now realised that more people were behind them, backed up into the hall, black people, or black people of various shades, and white people too, hippie types. By the time they had lined themselves up with the others there were at least twenty people in the room.

Listen, all of you, said Payley, beginning to raise his voice, I sympathise with what you're doing here, I understand the concept of prior ownership, I'm not stupid, but you're going boots and all into something you really don't understand. There are *processes*, comrades, which everyone has to go through. I've just explained this to Uncle here. The colour of your skin or the shape of your eyes, this doesn't matter; there are forms you have to fill in and sign, documentation you have to provide, payments you have to make. I'm sorry, but the state government is making nearly fourteen thousand dollars stamp duty out of the sale of this place: who here is going to come up with that sort of cash? You have to do the paperwork, he said, if you want to get anywhere in this world.

A couple of other protesters had straggled in and joined the semicircle behind and to either side of Bartleby. Payley was still sitting cross-legged on the floor, doing what he thought was the right thing, communicating face to face with the elder, but with all the others standing up—there must have been about thirty in the living room now—he was starting to feel that whatever authority he had was being leached out of him to the point where these people, quite clearly harmless in themselves, now felt like a threat. He looked into their faraway eyes and seriously thought they might spear him. He got to his feet—a badly executed stagger—so he could look at them on the same level. But, having done so, he realised he was now towering above Bartleby who, since he'd said that thing about not getting up, had neither spoken nor moved.

Almost instantaneously, Payley felt thirty pairs of eyes looking down at the back of Bartleby's head as if they were asking him: Is this okay, this guy lording it over you like that? I'm standing up, said Payley, gesturing with his arm to the group and at the same time tilting his head sideways in the direction of Bartleby, because I need to stretch my legs. I had an operation a little while ago and it's still playing up. He tapped the knee in question. So. I'm actually talking to you all. He swept an arm out in front to show them what he meant. Of course I empathise with you, he said, but what I'm saying at the same time is that you have to go about these things the right way. You can't just barge into someone's house and take it over. Where would the world be if everyone did that any time they liked? We've got to find a way to live together, even if we don't necessarily like each other all that much; the important thing is to overcome our differences, see what unites rather than divides us, if we are to live in a harmonious society, as we would like to do. That's why we have laws, he said, so we don't scratch each other's eyes out.

Now, he continued, I believe from what I have been told by your lawyer and from the few words Uncle has spoken that you as a group wish to claim ownership over the land on which this house is built and that you feel some entitlement, as indigenous people, to be gathered here as you are in this living room with its marble benchtops and state-of-the-art space-saving cabinetry, today. But *quicquid plantatur solo, solo cedit*; whatever is annexed to the soil is given to the soil, as our whitefella law has it. *Quicquid plantatur*: whatever is annexed. Can you as indigenous people enjoy ownership of the land here without *ipso facto* claiming ownership over the house and *ipso facto*, therefore, enjoying it? The house was not here when your forebears walked the land, so why should you now benefit from its comforts? We can't turn the clock back to a time when we and our houses and cars and shopping centres and shopping bags were not here and we shouldn't even try. We need to find a way forward. One that doesn't look back. I am absolutely an advocate for inclusion, Payley said, of having all peoples share in the wealth of a lucky society, but inclusion means just that, it means playing by the rules, doing your bit, you can't have one without the other.

I recently, said Payley, continuing, had an Iraqi man come into my office to plead his case to be allowed to stay. Who do you barrack for? I asked. He didn't understand 'barrack', I'm not sure he even understood 'for'. Do you see what I mean? You will always find me out there front and centre supporting multiculturalism, an *inclusive* society, but you will also hear me saying—I don't apologise for it—that everyone has got to pull their weight. Nothing is God-given, we're all in the same struggle against circumstances, we're all trying to make something better of our lives. My mum and dad couldn't afford to send me to uni, I had to pay my way, I worked two, sometimes three jobs, crammed my study in where I could. I struggled like the next guy but I accepted the struggle. The laws of the land are always about finding compromise, listening to both sides of the argument, making judgments based not on emotion but fact. There is a young couple currently living at home with the man's parents, the young woman seven-and-a-half months pregnant with their child, in despair at what is happening here and how their ownership of this house, as written and signed into the contract of sale, is being questioned.

It was hot in the room. The midday sun was beating down on the roof and streaming in through the glass doors. The heat and odour from thirty bodies meant the air in the living room had become almost unbreathable; sweat was dripping off Payley's forehead and had soaked the underarms of his suit jacket. The group were all sweating too, and those at the back in the direct sun were shading their heads with their hands. The only one who seemed to have stayed cool was Bartleby: his face had just a slight extra sheen. He had been listening to Payley throughout with his ear cocked, but now, on his forehead, otherwise as passive as stone, the backbencher could see a little furrow. On the brows of a few others, too, there were lines. The kids down the front were staring up at the man in the suit with their mouths open. They greatly respected their elders, and Uncle in particular—otherwise, no doubt, they would be outside playing. They were all waiting to see if the man in the suit had finished.

But now, said Payley, enough of me. It is time for Uncle to speak.

Payley had only ever met one or two Aboriginal people in his life, he was inner-city born and bred, and he didn't really know how he should address them. He'd been parachute-preselected into and won by a nearly twenty per cent majority a safe outer-suburban Labor seat—there was as much chance of running into a blackfella out there as there was of meeting a Kalahari bushman. He gestured for Uncle to speak. There was a long silence. Uncle, he said, you may speak.

Uncle's lips barely moved. Now I've sat down, he said, I won't be getting up.

Well, said Marshall, I'm sure you're all thinking that the next thing Payley did was call in the cops and get some heads kicked to save face—that's what we blokes do, don't we? Actually, that's what he should have done. In fact, what he did next was I'm sure against his better judgment. There was a clear right and wrong—the young couple were right, the squatters wrong—but the backbencher chose to take on Bartleby's cause.

He started defending him in the press, arguing the point with the outraged new settlers who came trooping into his electoral office (*If you let this happen once, it won't stop!*), took it up with his party colleagues and tried to get parliamentary support. He always ran the line—he had to—that while he didn't necessarily agree with their methods, we as a community couldn't completely ignore what they had to say. Maybe we were trampling over sacred ground a little too quickly and unthinkingly. Shouldn't we at least stop for a minute and draw breath? Look at the circumstances? Launch an enquiry? Payley kept visiting the house—the press were camped there, he knew there'd be photos—to sit down and parley with Bartleby and try to get something else out of him. He couldn't. He began to feel like everything he was doing—let's face it, risking his career—was for no other reason than to get Bartleby to speak and somehow 'explain himself'.

Then the young Indian wife had her baby and the photo was published on the front page of the papers. *Shock! Outrage!* An unwashed rabble were living in the house that was rightfully theirs, while they—now with a newborn—slept in the husband's parents' spare room. The tide turned against Bartleby and his supporters, including, and most dramatically, Payley. He was hauled in by the party and given a dressing down: a recent poll showed voter support plummeting in his aspirational lower middle-class electorate. He took their advice and stepped away. Shortly after that the cops raided the house, broke up the protest and arrested the occupants, including Bartleby. The house was restored at the government's expense to its original condition, the tradesmen returned to finish it off and there were plenty more happy snaps and smiley footage when the young couple and their baby moved in.

The case got dragged through the courts for a while but in the end the charges were dropped. Bartleby disappeared and, aside from a few stuttering attempts to revive the movement, his supporters disappeared too. Payley tub-thumped pretty strongly after that for the little guy, the battler, trying to pay his mortgage and put food on the table, while big government let welfare cheats get away with murder. His numbers crept back up again: at the next election he won by an increased majority.

Marshall placed the stick carefully back on the table.

It's about expediency, isn't it? said Evan. Don't you think? The quick fix. Keep it simple, stupid. We don't want to take time, get our hands dirty. Oh no! Do you see what I mean? We've become very good at avoiding the messy bits, haven't we? It's always someone else's problem. But what can we do, people? Seriously? What can we do?

It was only after he went on like this for a while that everyone realised Evan was pissed. Actually, everyone was a bit pissed but it was only Evan who was jumping out of his chair. Adam watched him, smiling.

Marshall sat forward. You're right, Ev, he said, it's true, and not just with politics but with everything. We're becoming short-sighted, stupid. Pretty soon even one plus one will be too complicated for us. Debate's a thing of the past—don't talk to me about debate! We only pay lip-service to it now. How many times already in this job would I have liked to undo a decision I'd made only because there was pressure to make one? We need to find time to relax, people, to sit down and have a chat, or soon we'll all be going over the cliff.

Absolutely, said Evan—but with that, in an instant, he seemed to have expended his last bit of energy. Marshall waited—but Evan had nothing left. Thunder rumbled above the house. That was a good story, said Megan. Everyone went quiet. Marshall sank back into the cushions. The pot bell went off. Megan got up.

They started organising dinner, an Italian-style casserole with the lamb loin chops Lauren and Adam had brought for a Saturday barbecue. There would be no barbecue now. They had onions, garlic, carrots. A tin of tomatoes. Dried herbs from the top of the cupboard. Half a bottle of wine. For a while there was some dispute about how much to put in: Adam, Evan and Marshall argued a splash, Megan said they'd need at least a cup to give it flavour. Marshall said he thought he might have a couple of bottles, a gift from a donor, in the back of his car—but then they looked out at the rain. Scissors, paper, rock, said Evan. I've got one, said Adam. What? said Lauren. A spare bottle, in my bag, wrapped in a jumper, just in case—it's a good one too. Now he tells us! said Evan. Adam went to get it.

Hannah was still looking out the window. God, she said—and she flicked on the outside light.

A river of water was pouring over the embankment onto the driveway, dragging a slurry of dirt and gravel and splashing around the wheels of the cars. Marshall's, at the end, had been cut loose. They watched, amazed, their faces pressed against the glass, as it floated across the road on a brown river of water and dropped into a shallow ditch on the other side. Fuck! said Marshall. He grabbed the real estate section from the couch, held it over his head, opened the balcony door and ran out.

It was not just the end of the driveway gone, half the front garden had been washed away too.

Then it went dark. Shit! said Adam, from the hallway. What? said Evan, looking round. Shit! said Adam, again. The only light was the glow from the fire. Are there candles? asked Hannah. Someone lit one. Hello? Tilly's here, said Adam. What? There was a silver light coming up the stairs, shaking and shivering. Everyone? said Adam—I think I can see Tilly here.

Tilly turned off her phone so the candle was lighting her. There's grog here somewhere for sure, said Evan, from the kitchen. Tilly? said Marshall, from the balcony door. The newspaper had moulded itself to his head. The lights are out, said Tilly. I got the wine, said Adam, holding it up. Tilly flipped her phone over and over in the palm of her hand. Whisky! said Evan. I found whisky here!

They lit more candles, set the table. Marshall? Evan poured some whisky into a glass with pictures of Bart Simpson on it. Marshall had taken the newspaper off but his hair was still stuck to his scalp. Tilly was in the living room on the couch, fiddling with her phone. (It was doing their heads in, that silver light; they were like moths, flapping around it but not getting too close in case it burned them up.) The pot bell went off and Hannah got up to empty it. Anyone else? said Evan, and he presented the whisky to each in turn.

Lauren set the casserole dish on a chopping board in the centre of the table. Adam opened the wine. Hannah brought in plates, knives and forks. It was, unexpectedly, a candlelit dinner. Are you going to have something to eat? asked Lauren. Come on love, said Megan. Tilly came to the table and sat at the place set for her, next to her father. Now we are eight! said Evan, raising his glass. No-one laughed. Maybe you should turn it off? said Leon. He spoke quietly, almost under his breath. Tilly flipped the phone around once in her hand. When did you last charge it? asked Evan. He spoke like someone who needed to know but also wanted to make out like he didn't. This morning, said Tilly. Phew, said Evan. Turn it off now please, darling, said Marshall, while we're at the table. Tilly did. The room changed without the silver light.

I'm sorry to hear about your Uncle Rylan, said Hannah. That felt like someone had dropped a bomb and Tilly said nothing at first. He was a troubled young man, said Marshall, always had been, trying this and that but never really getting his life together. I guess he'd had it a bit too easy—but easy's not always the best, is it? Lauren started serving. I tried to help him, said Marshall, with money and all that, but he couldn't hold on to anything for long. I'm just telling the truth, Tilly, he said, turning to her. Your mother would agree, Uncle Rylan had some lovely traits but listening to good advice wasn't one of them.

He seemed to be warming to his subject—truth is, they

were all warming to the idea of dealing with the elephant in the room—when Tilly pushed her chair back, picked up her phone and stepped away from the table. If Uncle Rylan was stupid, she said, and maybe he was, then stupid's better than liar. She hesitated, held her ground. She looked like a loaded spring. And if you don't want to do anything, she said—she was talking to them all—then why don't you just *get out of the way*.

The phone torch came on. She followed it downstairs. The door below opened and closed.

I'll do it, said Megan. There was something cold, abrupt, about her voice. Marshall stiffened, but let it go. Megan picked up the plate that Lauren had prepared and with a candle in her other hand she made her way downstairs. They all stared at their meals. Evan started first, the others followed. When Marshall spoke it was like he'd decided to confess to the plate of food in front of him and that of all things available this was the one most likely to offer absolution.

He was giving me the shits, he said, so I yelled at him, that's all. I gave him a serve. He had it coming. He was a lazy, selfish little prick who'd never lifted a finger in his life. Jackie's parents are working-class-made-good; they did everything so their kids didn't have to do anything. But Jackie had a conscience, she studied hard, worked hard—you all know that—she never once leaned on her parents for money. We scraped together our own deposit, took out a mortgage, paid it off week by week like everyone else. We never asked for hand-outs. But not Rylan. He stayed home all through his twenties, they bought him a car, whatever he wanted—when he finally did move out they even bought him his own apartment. Simple, working-class people who had earned what they had by the sweat of their brows.

So Rylan moves out and fucks around, goes to bars, eats at good restaurants, buys the best clothes, has one girlfriend after another but nothing that lasts. He tries a few jobs and they don't last either. He's got a self-destructive streak. Flies off the handle, says stuff he shouldn't. And whenever he needs money he just rings the old man. Jackie was always too soft on him. We used to argue about him, and I tried to keep out of it, really I did. Tilly loved her Uncle Rylan. And why? Because Uncle Rylan was full of shit. He listened to the coolest music, wore the coolest clothes, seemed to be always where the action was. It started to get to me, it shouldn't have, I know; what Rylan provoked in me was a kind of alien feeling. I'm rusted on Labor, you know that, I'm about a fair go for all, we hold out the helping hand when it's needed, we don't do sink or swim. But this idea had lodged in my head that Rylan was a bludger—like my dad used to say—and that he needed to get off his arse, take responsibility for his actions, show some initiative. Some *enterprise*. There I was running a campaign and winning a seat on a platform of old-style community values and all the while, on the side, I'm preaching dog-eat-dog individualism to my wayward brother-in-law.

The pot bell rang. That's you, said Evan. Fuck it, said Marshall. I'll do it, said Evan, and he got up. Woo, I'm a bit pissed, he said.

Megan came back from downstairs and sat at her place: she said nothing, did nothing, held her thoughts.

Go on, said Hannah.

Anyway, said Marshall, too far into his explanation now to turn back, one day when Rylan was over I lost it with him. I cut into him pretty hard, saying how he ought to get off his backside and do something, that he couldn't keep living off his parents like this. He was actually pretty contrite; he didn't argue, he just listened with that hang-dog look he sometimes got and at the end he said: You're right.

Jackie and I talked after that, for hours actually. I apologised, said I knew it wasn't my business but all the same I thought she should have a word with her parents, that they were being weak with him, that I understood how he was her brother and all that but he needed to harden up. That ended up all right, that discussion, and later she mentioned to me how she'd spoken to her parents and she was pretty sure they'd taken it on board.

So a few months went past, continued Marshall, and things seemed to have settled down, although the truth is I was too busy to notice. I was running the campaign—doorknocking, shopping centre walk-throughs, baby-kissing—then after the election settling into my seat, getting the run of parliament, making sense of what I could and couldn't do. So far as I could tell, Rylan was doing okay, keeping his head down and not putting his hand out too much. And by now Jackie was going through stuff too, as you know, and I felt like I needed to protect her.

Then late last year, before Christmas, I got word that Rylan had found a new girlfriend, younger than him, an artsy inner-city type and they were burning up the bars and all that again. I never met her but I got the impression she liked the good life. Then one day a couple of weeks ago he turns up at his parents' with her asking for money to start a new business. She's a designer, apparently, and the idea is they're going to make quirky jewellery to sell at the markets.

Well. Because of the conversation Jackie'd had with them, the parents told Rylan and his girlfriend that they'd have to think about it, then they rang me for an opinion. I was in the middle of some big policy meeting and I didn't really have the time. But anyway. They asked what they should do: Rylan was asking for money to start a craft-jewellery business. I said well, sure, that's good, that's great, he's getting his act together—but I think he should match them dollar for dollar. The parents agreed and rang Rylan to tell him. So the next thing, of course, was that Rylan was ringing Jackie asking could she lend him a sum of money, which, I soon found out, was exactly half the amount he'd asked their parents for: the half, that is, that he was supposed to be contributing. She rang me. I said no, fuck him Jackie, I don't care who he is, make the little shit go out and find his half himself, that's the least he can do. Jackie took my advice and rang Rylan—and after that the whole thing went quiet. Then yesterday, Friday—is it Saturday? I'm confused—I'm in my office doing some work and Rylan comes in, on his own, without the girlfriend, and says he wants to talk. So I take him out the back and shut the door.

He's angry, but hipster angry; it doesn't really work. He says he thinks it's me behind the parents and Jackie not giving him any money and reminds me it was I who said he should stop slacking off and do something with his life and now I was blocking it. He was raising his voice. He said it was a pissy amount he was asking for compared to the money his parents and Jackie and I spent every day. It's not about the money, it's the principle, I said. That really set him off. He got all jumpy and started pacing the room and yelling. He kept saying how he'd tried, I didn't understand, Jackie and I had been to uni, got an education, walked into good jobs. But he was still lost, he said, had always been lost, the underachiever. Jackie was the special one and he knew he'd never measure up.

I could see the tears in his eyes. I know I'm useless, he said, but listen, Marshall, is making jewellery with my new girlfriend a lesser thing than what you're doing here? I didn't know what to say to that. *What the fuck was I supposed to say to that?* Every single human being, he said, every single human creature on this earth has got to be worth *something*—but you, you all think I'm worth *nothing*. You won't give me a chance. Just because I didn't finish uni, that means I'm a bludger, a slacker. Doesn't matter how much Mum and Dad or Jackie *love* me, the fact is they can't respect me. And respect is all I want, Marshall, to prove myself in your and everybody's eyes. It's a pissy amount of money, but you won't give it.

He opened his jacket. He'd strapped a piece of old computer circuitry to his stomach with electrical tape, wires and other bits sticking out. I could see right away it wasn't real. In fact, it was pathetic. (And this is the guy who wants to go into craft jewellery!)

It's a bomb, he says. He's sweating, shaking; it's almost like he's convinced himself it is. (Legal fiction! Ha!) And if I don't take him seriously we're both going off to meet our Maker. Then he starts bawling. I want to laugh, but instead I feel sick. The sight of him screwing up his face like that is literally making me nauseous. I let him go on for a bit then I walk out to the front office—there's a regular out there, an old Greek guy, Spiro, he's always got something on his mind. I say hello but sorry, I'm busy today. I tell my staff to take an early lunch. I have some family matters to attend to. Then I go back to my office. Rylan is in the chair, his jacket still open, snot running from his nose. I wait till I hear the front door close.

Marshall looked down at his plate, straightened his knife, aligned it with the fork.

I ripped into him, he said. I didn't hold back. I'd listened to everything he'd said but it was all piss and wind. The tears too, it was all an act. I tore shreds off him. I said this private enterprise stunt was a load of crap, it was just another excuse to bludge off his parents. If he was a loser, like he said, it was his own fault, no-one else's. And this? I said, pointing at the 'bomb'. Really? Did you *really* think I was going to buy that? I didn't stop. Once I'd emotionally beaten him to a pulp, I showed him the door, escorted him all the way to the front, told him to dry his eyes and zip his jacket, said I hoped he understood all I'd said was for his own good. Then I went back in and rang Jackie. I told her what I'd said, and why. She was upset, of course, but we talked, and things seemed to settle down. I said I thought we should still go away. Rylan would be fine. A weekend down the coast would do us good. I said I'd pick her up about four. Tilly would stay at her friend's. Three-thirty I got the call.

Everything went quiet.

You got down here with Tilly around nine, said Hannah, like she was clarifying something with herself. Yeah, said Marshall. Only—what?—five and a half hours after your brother-in-law committed suicide? Yeah, said Marshall, again. And you left Jackie at home, she said. Marshall nodded. Again it went quiet.

Well, said Megan, standing up and gathering the plates,

I don't know about you guys but I'm just about ready for the next story.

I've got one, said Adam, getting up.

Marsh, come on, forget it, said Megan. He hadn't moved. The timer went off. That's mine, said Lauren. Where's Evan? said Adam. They all looked around. He was at the top of the stairs, shoes off, clothes muddied and dripping, a stupid grin on his face, holding Marshall's two bottles of donor wine triumphantly over his head. It's still raining out there, he said. Everyone, even Marshall, laughed.

While Evan had another shower and changed they stoked the fire and lit more candles. It was freezing outside, and whale-belly black. The wind was wild. The rain relentless. No-one had forgotten the road was blocked and half the driveway gone or that Tilly was downstairs on her phone—but they tried to push it from them and move on. Two nights of stories: leave all the frenetic stuff behind, find a bit of quietness and order. But the plague was still out there. A sub-audible jangle creeping up through the floorboards—gossip, backstabbing, trumpet blowing, everyone talking over everyone else—that all the wine in the world wouldn't still.

Evan came back, shivered a moment, and started pouring. Megan poked the fire. The dishwasher hummed. The house groaned. The rain dripped into the pot.

All right, said Adam, picking up the stick. My story is called *Home*. I like that, said Hannah. It's sort of about real estate, said Adam. Evan raised an eyebrow and put the bottle down. It was something that made the papers, but not in a big way—if you recognise it don't go spoiling it for everyone else. I heard it from the defending lawyer; I was out having a drink with him and it came up during a conversation we were having about country-property prices and how tight the market is these days and how desperate some people are.

It's about a couple, like in Lauren's story. Heterosexual again. They were both well off, successful. Like Lauren's. But. No. Wait. I'll go back.

Adam: Home...

This couple were childhood sweethearts, you see, deeply in love. Their names were Cass and Dale. They'd gone to kindergarten together, then primary school, then secondary school, eventually even to the same business college. Their parents were old friends, and when they were little the kids would play games together from dawn till dusk, big rowdy games that nearly always ended in tears. The two families went camping at the same site every Christmas, and Cass and Dale would spend whole days in each other's company, damming the river with rocks, jumping off the rope swing into the big swimming hole. They played doctors and nurses. They never missed a birthday. They married in their early twenties and had their first kid shortly after. But the kid was disabled, severely disabled, and right from the start he needed around-the-clock care. But that was okay, they were both in good jobs, earning good money—Dale in IT, Cass in HR—and they could afford to pay. But the boy, Oscar, was very sick, and it was not the carer's fault when one day he swallowed his tongue, choked and died. So. You see.

Is this going to be another sad one? said Evan. Megan, sitting next to him on the couch, whacked him hard across the back of the head. Ow, he said. Everyone laughed.

All right, so, said Adam.

Naturally the first thing Cass and Dale did after they had mourned the loss of their poor little boy was to try and have another baby to see if they could fill the void. I can't imagine how it must have felt. But the trouble was, no matter how hard they tried, nothing happened. It was like God or whoever was saying you've had one and it turned out badly so no more for you now, okay? But they wouldn't give up. They tried all the natural methods, all the old wives' tales, everything, then they turned to IVF. There was no question, obviously, of them not being accepted into the program; as bargaining chips they had on the one hand the tragic death of their first child and on the other the argument that the procedural checks and balances would make sure they didn't have another like Oscar to break their hearts again.

But still Cass couldn't get pregnant. First it was her eggs, then it was Dale's sperm; then it was neither. At some deep level their genetic material just didn't want to get together; it had got together once and wasn't happy with the results. They gradually became resigned to their fate—although the medical profession, hell-bent on trying to help them, took a little longer to catch up. It was Cass who eventually called a stop; she knew her body better than anyone. Enough was enough. Dale felt the same. They were childless, and childless they would remain.

But the weird thing—and it was probably this that drove a lot of what happened next—was that once they stopped trying they became not only a childless couple but also a couple who for all intents and purposes *had never had one*. Oscar became a memory and barely that. His ashes were buried in a lawn cemetery way out in the sticks; for the first few months they visited the grave every Sunday and put flowers on it, but soon this ritual became less regular and then was abandoned. For the first few months, they kept his room the way it was, his bed still spread with his favourite stuffed animals, the *Toy Story* poster on the wall; pretty soon they'd not only stopped going in there but had even dismantled the shrine. Cass put the stuffed toys in a big black garbage bag, put that bag in the hallway, then a while later in the boot of the car, then a couple of weeks later, again, when she happened to remember it, into a charity bin. Oscar's room became the spare room; they piled their work papers on the bed, took down the *Toy Story* poster and put up a wall planner instead. It became the bits and pieces room, then by default the storeroom. If Cass saw a new set of crockery on special, for example, or a set of pure cotton towels, she would buy them and put them in there. They still called it Oscar's room, but it was no longer Oscar's room at all.

But the most liberating thing (for Cass especially, but Dale too) was that once they had grieved the loss of the child and accepted the fact of their childlessness they no longer needed to care about their bodies. During the restrained period of mourning over Oscar, then the strict regime of healthy eating and exercise imposed on them by IVF while they tried for a replacement, Cass and Dale had become puritans. She owned a library of healthy-eating books; he, to increase his chances of producing healthy and plentiful sperm, had given up drinking and installed a running machine in the garage.

The first sign that this regime and their pursuit of a second child was over was when Dale one night brought home a bottle of good wine and suggested they drink it together. Cass didn't object. When they finished that bottle he went and got another. Something was released in them, like a knot unravelling, a flower blooming. At some point that evening, after the second bottle, they both seemed to have arrived at the same consolation; after all they'd lost they at least had each other.

It was the beginning of a new life. They would no longer be servants to Cass's empty womb, or the countless doctors and specialists and their well-meaning advice. After that first drought-breaking bottle they drank every night. Neither of them mentioned the taboo they were breaking, the sense of a great burden having been lifted or whether or not, in fact, their quest for another child was officially over. They talked about everything else: their childhood together, their teenage years, the million shared moments. *Do you remember this? And then that happened? And that?*

They became not just a childless couple but a couple who enjoyed their childlessness. Instead of the teetotal and high-protein diet they had punished themselves with for so long they became gourmands: even a weekday dinner for two was prepared to a recipe from a glossy book, shopped for separately with a detailed list and accompanied by a rare wine. Dale had become a collector; tasting obscure vintages was now his obsession. He'd scour the wine shops and the internet and keep the bottles he bought in racks in Oscar's room. Every night before eating he and Cass would taste that evening's chosen vintage and have a short conversation about it and Dale would make tasting notes in his little cloth-bound book.

Financially, they were doing fine. The quest to get Cass pregnant had not in any way interfered with their nine-to-five lives. The constant round of tests and consultations had been done out of hours or on coordinated sick days or RDOs. Dale was now IT manager for a big supermarket chain (and was being head-hunted by others); Cass was a change management consultant for hire with her own website and business card, specialising in redundancy and redeployment. They both earned good money, and, cut loose from their roles as would-be parents, were now determined to spend it. They put on a few kilos, but neither cared. If they weren't eating expensively at home they were eating even more expensively out; they went to the theatre, the cinema or a concert five out of seven nights a week. They outgrew their home, not with family but possessions. Cass had become a devoted online shopper—clothes, shoes, bags, homewares—while Dale's wine collection now numbered hundreds of bottles. They sold their house and bought a bigger one, a few streets away, but pretty soon all of its rooms were full too.

Dale's next hobby was cars. He'd never had any interest in them, other than as a practical method of getting to work and the shops, but now the idea of owning as many cars as he could became an obsession. His main thing was 1950s American convertibles. Every night after dinner he'd roam the net and sit in chat rooms, refining his knowledge, and then like a hunter track down and corner his prey. When Dale got notice that his latest purchase was waiting for him down at the docks Cass knew that the next weekend would be devoted exclusively to reading the manual, polishing it up and taking it out on its first drive.

Cass didn't mind Dale's obsession—she had obsessions

of her own, currently for collecting fashion eyeware—and the upside was that every weekend when the weather was warm they would take one of Dale's cars out of the enormous garage he'd had specially built and go for a drive in the country. No child, fit or flawed, could ever outdo the satisfaction to be got from seeing the envy on the faces of the people they passed. They did the gourmet trails mostly—east, north, south-west, wherever—and arranged the day around morning tea at a café, bakery or tearooms, lunch at a winery, some more wineries and tastings in the afternoon, then a farmgate stop for fresh produce on the way home. Pretty soon this weekend ritual marked the passage of their lives. The garage filled with cars, the cellar with wine, the pantry with produce, the spare rooms with stuff. They began to wonder—separately at first, then quietly, by small steps, together—if this was it, their lives? Professionally they were both at the top of the tree, materially they had everything they could want.

But spiritually? said Hannah. Everyone sort of rocked back in their chairs. Yes, said Adam, exactly. He took a sip of wine.

Then, he continued, coming back one day from a drive to the Yarra Valley in their new vintage Chevrolet convertible, Dale slowed down on a straight stretch of road near Coldstream and pulled onto the verge. What are you doing? asked Cass. Dale pointed at the paddock to their left.

It was a Sunday in autumn, about four o'clock in the afternoon, the sun was low and the light was starting to change. It was doing that thing it does where it fades from the sky but picks out the things on the ground until they seem almost to glow—it's a beautiful time that, isn't it?

The verge was wide, beside it a grassy culvert then a barbed-wire fence. There were plenty of new wineries dotted along that road but this part was still old farmland and now, at milking time, what Dale was pointing at was a herd of black-and-white cows making their way up the rise towards the milking shed next to an old farmhouse tucked in behind some trees.

Dale and Cass got out of the car, leaned on it and watched. There was something unearthly about the scene. Time had slowed, they were on the moon and those cows were weightless, floating towards the shed on a gentle solar breeze. They could see the farmer standing up there, the cows floating towards him; behind the herd a dog swept back and forth across the grass like a scythe. There was nothing sharp or violent about it, the dog didn't even bark, it too was gliding, like on the moon, or underwater. There was a golden sheen on everything, the black hides of the cows, the clear earth around the shed, the shed itself, the farmer's shoulders. Clouds of golden insects rose up out of the grass as the cows passed and in the wake of the scything dog.

As Dale and Cass watched all this an otherworldly calm

descended on them. Their lives seemed concentrated and distilled. Cass moved her hand to his and held it like she was saying: Do you feel it too? He squeezed it lightly like he was saying: Yes. Ahead of them, along the road, on top of the wire fence, three ravens sat watching. They too felt the calm. I want that, said Dale. Cass knew exactly what he meant. Dale thought he saw the farmer wave his hand and he raised his hand too. Let's go up, he said.

It was the sort of road—more a track, really—on which Dale, under any other circumstances, wouldn't be seen dead driving his new Chevrolet convertible. It was rutted with tractor tyres and the chassis scraping along the rise in the middle. But an idea or a feeling towards an idea had taken hold of Cass and Dale and silently they both agreed that a few scrapes on the undercarriage were a small price to pay to discover where this feeling might take them.

When they got to the top of the track the farmer wasn't there but they could hear the mooing and bellowing and the clatter of hooves inside the shed. The milking had started. Dale closed the Chevrolet's roof. They got out and went to the door—not a door, really, more an opening through which the cows had trooped. Everything in there was the opposite of what they'd felt outside; it was busy, noisy, cows lurching and moaning, metal gates clanking, the farmer whistling and shouting, the dog barking and music blaring from a tinny radio hanging above on a wire. The farmer was getting what must have been about twenty of the herd individually into the corrals on the big milking carousel—the others were penned in a concrete yard at the far end, waiting their turn. While the dog barked—routinely, and less frequently now—the farmer, an old guy in his seventies, went around to each cow and attached the milking cups to their udders, oblivious to the two well-dressed professionals from the city standing in the doorway of his shed. Or so it seemed. Hello there! he said, from the other side of the carousel, and he walked around towards them. Can I help you with something?

It was an odd sight, said Adam, the two city types standing either side of a cow pat, their flash car in the yard, while the farmer approached in his gumboots and waterproof pants and filthy flannel shirt. The dog came round the other side, its ears up, curious.

We were watching from the road, said Dale—I saw you, said the farmer—and we couldn't help coming up for a look. They're so beautiful, said Cass, and they look so calm and peaceful from a distance. Mostly they are, said the farmer, but they get a bit cranky sometimes—don't we all? Everyone smiled. My name's Gus, said the farmer. Dale and Cass, said Dale. That's a beautiful-looking vehicle, said Gus, pointing at the Chevrolet. I collect them, said Dale. The farmer let out a breathy whistle. It's a hobby, said Dale. An expensive hobby, said Cass. They all smiled again. Does it hurt the cows? asked Cass. The farmer looked around. No, he said, it becomes habit after a while. Do you ever milk them by hand? asked Cass. Oh no, said the farmer, we haven't done that in a long time, but you can, sure, with the placid ones. Bess there is as gentle as a kitten. Can I try? asked Cass. Both Dale and the farmer looked at her, surprised. Sure, said the farmer: why not?

With the dog at his heels, Gus moved to the pen, opened the gate and pushed a couple of cows aside until he got a hand on what even Cass and Dale, urban amateurs, could see was the most placid of the group. Pushing her gently by the back of the head (Dale remembered the principal at school doing this, when he was taking kids to the office), Gus guided Bess onto the open concrete area. Just hang on to her for a couple of minutes, said Gus, while I get the next lot in. He parked Bess beside Cass and showed her how to put a hand on the cow's neck to steady her, then he went back to the carousel and started unhooking the others and shooing them into the paddock. Then one by one he hooked the next lot up.

Bess didn't move. Cass could feel the warmth of her body through the hide and the occasional twitch of a muscle deep under the skin. The odour coming off her—of grass and straw and milk and piss and shit and something else that she couldn't help somehow thinking was old timber—made her reel at first but soon became a pleasant thing, like nature talking, the same as the picture from the roadside of the herd making their way up the paddock in the gloaming. Subtly Cass patted Bess's hide, but so subtly that if you weren't looking for it you wouldn't have seen it. Bess turned her head, one big eye bulging.

All right, said Gus, wiping his hands on his shirt and picking up an old milk crate on the way over, so what brings you people out here today? He put the crate down. Bess shuffled on the concrete. Are you sightseeing? We had lunch in a winery up near Healesville, said Dale, and now we're on our way home. You live in the city? said Gus, kicking the milk crate into place. In the city, yeah, said Dale. And what do you do for a crust? asked Gus. Well, said Dale, I'm in information technology, Cass does human resources. Stressful work, yeah? said Gus. Most times, said Dale. Sometimes the city looks like one big ball of stress to me, said Gus. Whenever I go there— and I try to avoid it if I can—I feel like a hundred strangers are whacking me with sticks. No, I couldn't live in the city, he said, but hats off to those who can.

The whole time Gus was talking he was tapping the milk crate with his foot, this way and that, nudging it into position. Bess seemed to know what was coming, a memory somewhere deep in her genes, and she grew a little skittish. Cass said nothing, but gave all her concentration to the hand stroking Bess's neck. She was calming the cow down, but also herself. Little by little Bess's hooves stopped shuffling and Cass's excitement—where did that come from? what was its source?—began to subside.

All right, said Gus, sit down, let her get used to you

first, I'll get a bucket, wait a sec. Cass sat on the milk crate, spread her knees and put her hands on Bess's side. Dale stood above her. Cass let him take in the picture of her like that, sitting on the milk crate, her legs spread, her hands on the cow, before she looked up and smiled. They smiled at each other, and both knew it was the kind of smile they'd not felt in a very long time.

Gus put a blue plastic bucket under the cow. All right, he said, you've probably seen how they do it in the movies— I mean, it's not rocket science. You get a teat in each hand, aim at the bucket, then squeeze and pull down. Cass did what Gus said. That's right, he said, squeeze and pull, keep going, it'll start in a minute, I need to get this other lot off the machine, keep going, it'll start soon. Gus left them there— Cass squeezing and pulling Bess's teats, Dale watching—while he disconnected the cows already milked, herded them out into the paddock and brought the new ones in. Cass and Dale were left alone. The background sounds seemed to fade—the clatter of hooves, the clanking of gates, the cows moaning, the machine humming, Gus whistling and calling, the radio on the wire—until all Cass could hear were Bess's hooves shifting, her tail flapping, the squeezing, like when you wring your hands together, flesh on flesh, her own breathing, and now, finally, the sound of a squirt of milk hitting the bottom of the bucket.

It felt miraculous at first, then somehow ordinary. Once

Bess had let the milk down—and Cass could actually feel her relax—the milking seemed to manage itself. The tiniest squeeze, the slightest movement of the wrist, and out shot the stream of white liquid. Cass glanced up once at Dale and smiled—a girlish smile of the kind he'd not seen since they were, in fact, boy and girl—then gave herself over to it. She leaned her forehead against Bess's side, for a while she even closed her eyes so she could listen more closely to the sound as it now was of liquid squirting into liquid. She aimed one teat slightly sideways so that it squirted at her hand. She did the same to the other, so that now as she milked she felt the milk softening her skin, letting her fingers slip easily up and down over the teats. This seemed to relax Bess even more. The bucket now had a couple of centimetres of milk in the bottom, the squirting sound had gone from high to low, the milk seemed to be pouring out of Bess with Cass barely moving her hands.

That's the way, said Gus, coming over. Look at you, you're an old hand. And to Dale: She looks like she's been doing it for years. Good girl, he said, to Bess, stroking her rump, good girl. Cass looked up at the farmer and in that moment Gus saw like Dale not a woman but a girl. Good on you, he said, that's a good litre or more there now. Let me get you something to put it in.

Gus went back to the house. Dale wandered over to the carousel to watch the other cows being milked, then moved to the doorway at the far end of the shed and looked out across the farm. Cass stopped milking for a moment and watched him. The machinery hummed. She lifted her milky hands to her face, smelled them, then rubbed the milk into her skin. She closed her eyes and kept rubbing. It was like at the bathroom mirror in the morning except here there weren't the usual smells of soap and product but milk, grass, cowshit, cowhide, concrete. Cass rubbed until she felt the milk going in then opened her eyes and stared down at the bucket.

Gus came back with a big glass jar, the kind you might buy olives or pickles in. He stood next to Cass and unscrewed the lid. Give us the bucket, he said, you can take it home in this, it'll last a while if you keep it in the fridge. Cass handed up the bucket, Gus put the jar on the ground and poured the milk into it. Cass got up off the milk crate and, before moving away, wiped her hands a couple of times on Bess's side. The hide was warm and seemed to shiver. Dale? she said. Gus screwed the lid on the jar.

Outside the sky had darkened, a few pink clouds and a soft glow in the west. Cass was carrying the jar. Thank you, she said. She slid into the passenger seat and Gus closed the door. Cass wound down the window. That was lovely, she said. No problems, said Gus. Thanks, said Dale, leaning down and looking across. Safe driving, said Gus. The tyres crunched on the gravel. Dale flicked the lights on. Cass turned to watch Gus walking back towards the milking shed and then, when she couldn't turn any more, she swung around and looked out the front where the headlights were throwing a tunnel of white onto the darkening road.

Shit, said Marshall. What's going to happen? said Megan. *Something's* going to happen, said Hannah. Good stuff, said Evan. All right, said Adam: so.

The following Sunday afternoon, just as the cows were heading up the hill, Gus saw Cass and Dale's Chevrolet making its way along the drive. We hope you don't mind, said Cass, getting out, but it was so wonderful, last week, we haven't stopped talking about it. Can Dale have a go this time? Sure, said Gus, come in. They went inside while Gus got the first of the herd into the carousel then, like before, led Bess with a hand on her neck towards them. She seemed to know what was required and stopped still without twitching. The bucket's over there, said Gus, you know what to do. Let me get the rest of these up. He crossed to the door on the far side and went out where the cows were gathering; Cass and Dale could hear him whistling to the dog and the clump and clatter of the cows' hooves. Bess didn't move. Cass kicked the milk crate over then went and got the bucket. She put it down under Bess's udder and laid a hand on her side. All right, she said, relax. If you're relaxed, she's relaxed, and if she's relaxed she'll do it for you. Dale wiped his hands on his jeans and started milking.

After a while Gus came over to see how they were getting

on. Good on you, he said. Then he and Cass watched while Dale pulled down on the teats and the milk fired into the bucket.

Next Sunday, when the car pulled up in the yard, it was only Dale who got out. Cass's not feeling well, he said, but I thought I'd come anyway. Gus hesitated this time before he led him into the shed. Stay here, said Dale, when Gus started to walk away, I want to make sure I'm doing it right. Gus stood and watched while Dale pulled down on the teats. Bess shuffled on the concrete; Dale adjusted the bucket. Then the pulling resumed. Dale looked up at Gus who, shifting and distracted, said he needed to go and deal with the cows.

The next Sunday Cass was feeling better and they both took it in turns to milk Bess. While Cass was milking Dale cornered Gus. Did he make a living? Had he thought about running other animals? A vineyard? Did he have a wife? Kids? Gus answered each one but after a while he began to feel uncomfortable, he had a lot of things to do, he said, and while he appreciated their visits and their interest in the farm he was actually a very busy man, running the whole thing on his own, working seven days a week.

The next Sunday they made an offer. They didn't go straight into it. After talking about it during the week they agreed they would have to play their cards carefully if they weren't to lose Gus's friendship. They arrived a bit earlier, around lunchtime. Dale started by saying they were sorry for having already taken up so much of Gus's valuable time—as nine-to-five city people their Sunday was a day of rest and they hadn't yet grasped that for a farmer Sunday is like any other day and that there is always work to be done. So, said Dale, as you can see, we haven't come winery-hopping but have put on our work clothes and are here to help out: you only have to tell us what to do.

Gus was taken aback by this offer, naturally, but he couldn't send them away. He thanked them and gave them some simple chores, like cleaning out the old shed. Cass and Dale made two piles, one big, one small, the first with things that in their opinion had no imaginable use, the second with things that looked like junk but which Gus might like to keep. The light turned, the sky faded to pink, the insects came out, the birds started roosting, the cows pushed their way into the yard while the dog swept the ground behind them. Cass and Dale stopped and poured themselves a cup of tea from their thermos and took a biscuit each from the bag. Gus came over. Well! he said. Behind them one of the cows was bellowing. All three realised it was Bess.

Cass did the milking this time while Dale talked. He let Gus understand that he and Cass had fallen in love not just with Bess and the milking but the whole thing, the farm, the lifestyle and everything that went with it; they had, further-more, come to see Gus as a friend. This was the basis of their offer, which by any measure, said Dale, was over-generous. He quoted a figure. We want to buy the farm from you, he said.

This offer is for everything: land, house, sheds, machinery, livestock. It is generous, Gus, very generous; I don't think we need to haggle.

A little cog went clunk in Gus's brain as he listened to Dale and thought back on nearly two months of Sunday visits from this sweet but strange city couple. They'd been massaging him, getting him ready, for this. No, he said, stepping back, not daring to look up. I'm sorry, this is my life, I'm a farmer, it's my family's land, I'm staying, no offence, thanks, but no.

All three went quiet. The cows mooed and clattered, the machinery hummed and clicked.

Sorry, said Gus.

Undeterred by the farmer's rejection of their offer, Cass and Dale came back the following Sunday and offered more. This time Gus really was creeped out, not least by the fact that in order to sweeten things Cass had brought as a gift a freshly baked carrot cake in a tin with a red ribbon around it. Gus took it from her—he even ate a slice that evening after dinner—but again shook his head. When Dale—something white-hot brewing in him—upped the offer on the spot by another hundred thousand, Gus backed away. Please, he said, I told you, I don't want to sell.

The following Sunday Gus retreated into the milking shed when he saw the car coming up the drive. He wasn't well. He'd woken the previous Monday feeling awful, struggled to get the milking done, vomited all day, then struggled again through the evening milking and had gone to bed early, pale and sweating. It was the same on Tuesday too. When the car pulled up in the yard he came out of the milking shed waving his arms and shouting: No, no, not today, not any more, I can't do it, please! Cass stayed in the passenger seat; Dale stood behind the driver's door. We've had a think, he shouted back, we're going to raise the offer by a third! We will give you three million dollars for the property which is *twice* its market value! Gus waved his arms again and violently shook his head. It was almost like he was trying to dislodge the three million dollar offer, the couple, and the last two months of Sundays from it. *No, please!* he said, and he walked back inside.

I suppose I don't need to tell you, said Adam, that Cass and Dale were the kind of people who were used to getting what they wanted. They'd already tried to poison Gus. There was arsenic in the carrot cake, Cass had bought it over the net, but now that he'd refused their three million dollar offer they would need to take further steps. Later that Sunday, after dark, they drove back out to the farm and parked on the verge. Cass kept lookout; Dale approached on foot. When the dog came towards him, ears up, he called quietly to it and took the little plastic container of meat from his jacket. The dog wolfed it down. Dale continued on up to the house. The back door was unlocked. Gus was snoring. Dale checked all the windows were closed then turned the taps on the gas stove up full. He crept back down the driveway in the moonlight. The dog followed him for a while, sniffing, hoping for more food, and Dale had to shoo it away. It stood at the gate and watched the Chevrolet, lights out, drive slowly back to the main road.

Gus woke up feeling awful, but very much alive. He threw open all the windows and doors. It seemed nothing could kill him. When Cass and Dale pulled up on the side of the road at the bottom of the hill (they'd both taken the day off work), they watched what should have been a dead body backing the tractor out of the shed and driving it around the other side of the hill to work on the fences there. They watched, too, when the tractor returned and Gus walked up to the house for lunch. Later he backed his ute out and drove it down the driveway past them, then off along the road into town. Of course he knew they were watching, they knew he knew, but neither of them flinched. That night Dale poured a can of petrol onto the bushes below Gus's bedroom window. When the dog came to greet him it got poisoned meat. But Gus was awake. Very awake. He got the extinguisher to the fire before it had even scorched the paint. He found his dog next morning, white froth around its mouth, and buried it under the persimmon tree down the side.

On Wednesday Dale, without Cass, drove the Chevrolet brazenly up the drive. Gus was in the milking shed with his shotgun. Dale called out: Gus, please, we're sorry! Gus, are you there? Listen, please, we need to talk! Gus stood at the door with the weapon ready. It was strange, thought Dale, with no dog around to sniff your ankles. Gus, please, he said, that's not necessary, I'm here to talk, I need to explain. Please. Gus lowered the gun, but kept his finger ready.

I don't want to talk to you, he said, I've got nothing to say; I'm not selling the farm, I've made that clear, you'll need to kill me, I know you've tried. No-one has the right to make me go. I don't care about your money, you can wave it around all you like. It might work for your city friends but it doesn't work for me.

Dale could hear the cows mooing in the shed. He thought about Bess, his hands on her teats, and felt a hot, anxious sensation. He thought about Cass and how much he loved her. Please Gus, he said, you've got no idea, I know what all this means to you—he gestured to the rolling green hills—but you've got to understand what we've been through. We're not here because we want to annoy you, or upset you, or even hurt you. We're here because we're lost, we're desperate, Gus, we're bereft. We had a kid, a beautiful little child, but he had stuff wrong with him, everything was wrong with him for God's sake, he choked on his own tongue. We tried to have another—we tried and tried and tried—but it didn't work. Our lives were wrong—while everything looked right on the surface, there was a great river of wrongness underneath.

Then we came here. A moment of chance. We never planned to own a farm, to be farmers, to milk cows, make cheese, grow vegetables, fruit. But we've realised there is nothing else that will heal the deep wound. We want to live a simple life, like you. We believe simplicity will save us.

Gus looked at him almost condescendingly, took his finger off the trigger and let the shotgun hang. You people think you're so important, don't you? he said—like your problems are the only problems anybody ever had. Did you ever stop to ask did I have problems? Did I have a wife? A kid? Was I happy? Yes, all three. Once.

I don't give a fuck, said Dale. My life is worse than yours—look! Dale gestured again to the rolling green hills so Gus would not mistake what he meant. Yes, said Gus, and when I die it will go to my daughter-in-law and her kids, not you. Dale felt that anxious sensation under his skin again but this time it was cold, not hot. Gus must have sensed it, and he raised the gun a little. There was a huge, tortured bellow from one of the cows in the shed. Instinctively, Gus turned towards it. Dale moved fast to the clutter of junk and put his hand on a piece of pipe. Gus still had the shotgun hanging. Dale flew at him from behind and bashed him across the head. Gus fell, moaned, and struggled for a moment to get up. But Dale bashed him again. He bashed him twenty, maybe thirty times. When he was sure he wasn't moving he dragged the body around the side and hid it under a sheet of iron. Then he went back and hosed down the blood.

It was not until a week later when a local farmer was driving past and saw Gus's cows bustling and moaning outside the milking shed that the alarm was raised. The farmer went up for a look and Dale came out to greet him. He was dressed in new gumboots, workpants and a checked flannel shirt. He explained to the farmer how Gus had retired—Dale and his wife, Cass, owned the farm now. They were still learning the ropes, of course, said Dale, smiling, but they'd be on top of it soon. He looked flushed. The farmer went away.

The next day a local cop, Senior Constable Matthews, came to visit and found Dale dragging a dead cow with a tractor and chain to a spot over on the far paddock where four other corpses already lay. They died, said Dale, without further explanation. Matthews started asking questions—way too many questions for Dale's liking—and then wondered aloud if he might perhaps see the contract of sale? I didn't know it was on the market, he said. Cass was watching from up at the house. Dale tried to look Matthews in the eye but it didn't really work. He said he didn't have the contract of sale on him right now but would have a look for it this evening and was happy for him to come back tomorrow.

Senior Constable Matthews went away, but he didn't come back the next day, he came back later that afternoon with another cop, a big guy called Stone. Cass came to the door in her apron and pointed to where Dale was dragging another cow onto the pile. The two cops picked their way across the paddock and asked him to turn off the engine. I haven't found the contract yet, said Dale. Matthews said this was not surprising since according to his enquiries the house had never been for sale. Would he like to explain? Dale put his arms on the steering wheel and rested his forehead on them. Cass turned back inside.

Later that afternoon more cops in blue overalls and white masks set to work, dragging the cows off the pile with the tractor and making another pile about twenty metres away. The stench was awful. When they got to the cow on the bottom they saw how her swollen stomach had been sewn up with bailing twine. They cut the twine and pulled. Gus's hog-tied body, stiff, bluish-white, slipped out from Bess's belly onto the mushy earth.

Ew! said Hannah. You're kidding me? said Marshall. That's fucked up, said Evan. Adam smiled. I'm a happy ending kind of guy, said Evan, you know that. I'm sensitive—a farmer getting hog-tied and hidden in a dead cow? I mean, come on, really.

So what happened, said Hannah, in the end? They were charged, said Adam, and jailed. The farm was sold, replanted; it's all vineyards now. That's really sad, said Lauren. Megan, who was sitting next to her, leaned over and touched her arm. It's the deep, deep yearning, isn't it, said Lauren, we've all got it, the need to fill the vacuum, with kids, a house, furniture, gadgets, *lifestyle*. But what happens when you take all that away? It's a dirty great gaping hole. And you're in freefall. Everything we do is part of this mad rush to fill the hole, plug it up, jump up and down on it just to make sure. We can't imagine what it would be like to have our lifestyles, our houses, our kids taken away—or we can imagine, that's the trouble, but we do everything we can to *not* imagine. Or—and here's the thing—because of the echo coming up out of that black hole every time we shout down into it we *throw it all away*, hurl it down there.

Adam looked at her. That's funny, said Marshall. They all waited, not knowing what to say. It's like this story I heard. Can I tell it? He took the stick off Adam.

Are we doing two? asked Evan.

Once upon a time, said Marshall—*What?* said Evan, looking around—there was this ex-County Court judge, an old soak, loaded to the gunwales with money, and this widow who lived on a farm. She would have been eighty, at least. So one day, the story goes (Marshall was already enjoying himself), the judge knocks on her door and offers to buy a portion of the farm, specifically the paddock with the low hill over the back. The judge has done some research and figured it might work for grapes. The old woman says sure, she's too old to do anything with it anyway. The judge plants a vine-yard. Years pass. The old woman gets older. The judge gets a viticulturist to look after his vineyard and this viticulturist divides it into seven parts so when the first grapes are picked and crushed he can compare the results. All the wines are good but one batch in particular stands out. In fact, it's spectacular—deep fruit, complex structure, lingering finish—and it soon becomes known in all the top wine circles as an absolutely stellar vintage. Even though the viticulturist is unsure exactly *why* this small patch of dirt is producing such extraordinary wine, he now puts all his energies into it and the wine becomes internationally famous. The widow is now very old, and she can no longer go out on the evening strolls she used so much to enjoy but sits by the window knitting or crocheting and thinking about the years gone by. (I'm enjoying telling this.) The judge comes to visit. He's brought his viticulturist with him. The viticulturist asks the woman why this particular patch might produce grapes of such superior quality? She seems reluctant to answer. The judge makes an offer—a very generous offer—for the rest of the farm. The viticulturist has figured out through the law of averages that there must be at least one more similarly stunning patch of *terroir* somewhere there. The woman goes silent, then launches into a diatribe: she has no time for the judge and his type, what would he know of the unspeakable suffering she has had to endure trying to make a living out of this heartless land? She raves on about her husband, her precious husband, and the cause of his death and how every evening after, crippled as she is, she would walk to that spot in the far paddock where their happy life came to an end. Barely four metres square. Yes, that's right, says the viticulturist. The size of an overturned tractor, says the woman, and underneath it my husband's mangled body. And there, says the woman, I would piss. The viticulturist looks shocked. Like a man, says the woman, proudly, spraying it all over the soil.

Everything went quiet again.

You get it? said Marshall. The woman's piss is what made that wine taste so good. All the geniuses in the world couldn't figure it out.

It's late, said Megan.

Everything influences what you end up with in the glass, said Evan, animated again: soil, climate, aspect. What affects the grape affects the wine. Well that may be true, said Leon, but even on my worst days I wouldn't drink something I knew had traces of old woman piss in it. Me neither, said Hannah. I'm going to bed, said Megan.

Doesn't matter, said Evan, waving an arm around: what's important is the flavour, the structure, the lingering on the tongue. It's old woman's piss! said Leon. Goodnight everyone, said Megan.

A while ago, said Evan, oblivious, there was this shiraz from Rockbank—ever been to Rockbank? I did a few jobs out that way once—which won this big wine competition. Rockbank! Dead paddocks, a few rocks, you wouldn't walk your dog there. Best shiraz in the world!

Balzac was married in Berdichev, said Adam.

But that's it, though, isn't it, said Marshall, on his own track, this notion of perfection, that we all have to be perfect. Aren't we all made of flesh, shitting, bleeding, puking flesh? That's the lie at the heart of it all, isn't it? Did that viticulturist tell his customers the main ingredient of his world-beating wine was *piss*. No, of course he didn't. He put it in the cellar, made it scarce, then five years later he released it at two hundred bucks a bottle.

The rain had stopped. Everything was quiet, save for the dripping in the pipes, out of the gutters, off the leaves. Marshall's car was still in the ditch, mud and bluemetal around its wheels. Clouds ran past the moon and out over the sea. A few stars were showing. The waves below curled and scurried, folding the moonlight in. Out at the skyline a ship passed—it had come from the far side of the world.

For fuck's sake, people, said Evan. Everyone's out there jumping off balconies and throwing themselves under trains, but we're good, aren't we? We're good. We've had a great day, a great night, we've got a great life. And I love you all. Which is why, he said, reaching awkwardly under the couch, I am going to share this bottle I found in the top cupboard and not keep it to myself!

He held a bottle of Cointreau aloft. Fuck, said Megan. She sat down again. Evan pulled the cork out with a squeak, reached across and offered it to Marshall. The Honourable

Member, he said. Marshall drank, and handed it to Lauren. The bottle went round: only Leon refused. It ended up back with Evan.

Greatest country on earth, he said, sticking the bottle between his legs. Twenty-one years of growth. *Australians all own ostriches!* Twenty-one-fucking-years of growth. What other good-rocking country on this big mother of an earth can boast *twenty-one years of growth*? It's true, said Marshall. I buy it yesterday, said Evan, I sell it today. Tomorrow I'm rich. It's true, said Marshall. I should be happy, said Evan. That's true too, said Marshall. So why aren't I? Meg? Why aren't I happy? Marshall took the bottle back. Evan sang: *Twenty-one today! Twenty-one today!* He laughed at his own joke. *Oh when the Saints! Go marching in! Oh when the Saints go marching in!* My guitar never comes out of the spare room. I don't go out eating, drinking, socialising, or when I do it's only because the money's burning a hole in my pocket and I need to prove that I can spend it on any damn fucking thing I like, throw it all off the tallest building, watch it flutter onto the peasants below. Aria's flown the coop. She loves me, I know that, she'll love me till I'm dead, but it was too much, living with us, with Megan's kids I mean, and all that competitive stuff going on. Sam's done well though, hasn't he? Meg? Sam's done well. But he's a pretentious arse. And now, today, this evening, my beloved Saints—excuse me, I'm going to cry—get walloped. And the whole fuckin' season's down the chute. By whom you ask? By *whom*? The Melbourne-fucking-Football-Club, that's *whom*. The Melbourne-fucking-four-wheel-drive-Mercedes-club, that's *whoom*. A sixty-nine-point shellacking.

He's right though, isn't he? said Marshall. We do live in the best country on earth. No-one answered that. But the trouble is, he said, pushing on, it's hard convincing people, isn't it? Everyone's so bloody negative. They can't see what they've got 'cause they think they're entitled to more. It's an entitlement problem, do you see? We've got this, so why can't we have that? And this and this and this?

Wait, said Adam. I was just saying, said Marshall. You brought your phone? Evan shrugged, flipped, flopped. You checked the footy scores? I don't believe this, said Megan. How? said Hannah. When I got the wine from Marshall's car, said Evan. You've got a lovely girl there, Marsh.

What? said Marshall. You broke the pact, said Megan. Oh Jesus, said Evan. No, you lied. A white lie, he said, completely white. You agreed with the rules, said Megan. I don't follow, said Marshall. He checked the scores, said Hannah, on Tilly's phone. Evan held his head in his hands. Oh man, he said.

Does it matter? said Lauren. What? said Megan. I just mean, said Lauren, there are lies and lies. I agree we should lighten up, said Marshall. There are big lies and little lies, she continued, good lies and bad lies, real lies and white lies, I don't think we should belt Evan up for using Tilly's phone. Megan was about to speak—*a weekend away, rediscover the real, drop down into some substance*—but she stopped herself, and sat back. You're right, she said. Evan looked at her. A light blinked on the horizon. Something crackled in the air.

Truth or Dare, said Marshall. What? said Evan. Come on, or just Truth. He was on the edge of the couch. That's stupid, said Lauren. We each tell a truth, said Marshall, the way we told a story. Could be good, said Megan. I'm into it, said Hannah. Adam? said Marshall. Adam shrugged. Lee? Leon nodded. I'm in, said Evan. Lauren looked at her fingers, fiddled with her rings.

All right, said Marshall, rearranging his politician's demeanour: we've told our stories, now we tell our truths.

Do we need a stick? said Evan. Marsh? Do you reckon we need a stick?

I made that whole story up, said Megan, about Abbie, and the road trip. She waved one hand over her eye, as if at a mosquito, then fixed on the painting like there was something in it yet to find. I worked it all out beforehand, so I could make it sound true. What? said Evan. His head was wobbling on his shoulders. When I was young, said Hannah, I guess about fifteen or sixteen, I used a shampoo bottle to, you know, and the top came off. My mother had to take me to the hospital. We were, like, half an hour waiting, at least, and then another hour on the trolley. I felt so embarrassed. All I could think of was what I would say when the doctor came and asked me what had happened.

Lauren? said Adam. I probably shouldn't have said that, said Hannah. Or didn't you even go to the Territory? said Evan, relentlessly, to Megan. I can tell you honestly, said Marshall, with my hand on my heart, that I always believed that what I was doing was for the best. Lee? said Lauren.

Leon hesitated.

Just before I retired, he said—his voice rang clear, he was the only one sober—I worked on this story about corruption in government. An open and shut case. A syndicate of brothel owners had been backhanding cash to this politician for years to get smooth passage on their permits. Then someone from inside started leaking. I met this woman, secretly, and she handed over a disk. We ran the story, named names. You might have read about it. The government got their attack dogs onto me, said it was a beat-up, denied everything and demanded I reveal my sources. I refused, but they wouldn't let up. They threatened me with proceedings. So one day my editor drags me into his office and tells me how things are getting difficult for him and that I might need to hang this public servant source of mine out to dry. It's just a few brothel permits, he says, it's not like it's a case of national security or anything. But I held out, held out longer than I should have. In the end my editor got on my back. Forget about the old code of ethics, Leon, he said, times have changed. If you don't name this woman, someone on a blog somewhere will. You're holding out for something but, mate, I'm sorry, it's already gone. He was very convincing, so I folded. I named my source.

A seabird squawked somewhere high above the house.

They found her two days later—a lovely woman, a husband, three kids—curled up in an old tree stump in the bush near Belgrave, an empty pill bottle in her lap. My boss felt bad, naturally. He offered me paid leave, a generous package. I mean, the paper had gone to shit anyway, everything was online, lead articles about paedophiles and gangsters and features on the history of the bra. The world had become nothing more than a tits-and-arse dance of tabloid revelation. What did I and my little secret matter?

He looked down. Hannah put a hand on his thigh.

You remember Dane? The director? In Aiden's story? He ended up doing that Dostoevsky thing. The title comes from that bit in the Bible where Jesus gets the demons out of a madman and puts them into a herd of swine. The swine all run over a cliff. It's like throwing away all the troubling stuff, you know, the stuff that sends you mad. But the trouble is, these days, we've got too many swine. It's all swine, you know? Everything's on the outside, there's nothing in the middle. Leon looked into the bottom of his glass. *We will rush, insane and raging*, he said, *from the cliff down into the sea.* I did good giving up drinking, it's been three years now. He put his hand on Hannah's thigh the way she'd put hers on his. Well, he said, that's me. Next?

Lauren shifted in her chair.

I fucked Leon, she said.

Adam was still catching up. So were the others, one by one. Leon and I fucked, said Lauren, after I had the operation, before he went out with Hannah. It wasn't planned, it just happened, and I thought it would be best not to tell.

You're fucking kidding me? said Adam. He looked at Leon. Leon looked at Lauren and hung his head.

Guys, said Marshall, I just want you to know, I have done everything I can. I have tried *so* hard, but everything, everything's gone wrong, I don't know how Jackie and I can stay together any more, I just don't, she wants my balls for breakfast, every morning, and I don't mean that in a good way. I shouldn't be saying all this, dumping all this stuff on you on this lovely weekend away. I've had a great time, really I have. You've been my friends, through good times and bad. Tilly hates me, I know that, she's off on her own trip now and there's nothing I can do. And now there's all this stuff going on at work. I mean I might have made a few mistakes—I'm not saying I haven't made mistakes—and maybe I've not always consulted properly, you know, but you've got no idea what it's like, every day, someone wants this, someone wants that, running around putting out spot fires and then when you turn your back for two seconds it's like a fucking conflagration. Rylan was white-anting me. It must have been him. Who else could it be? The slogans on the window, the rumours all over the net. Death threats. You've got no idea.

He uncorked the Cointreau and drank.

You mean to tell me, said Adam, ignoring everything Marshall said, that you've kept this from me all this time, even when I've gone on about him being a nice guy and how he's made mistakes but he's a good person at heart and one day he'll make a good woman happy? Forget it, Adam, said Lauren, it's not important now. What do you mean it's not important? he said, standing up. Let it go, she said. I'm sorry folks, said Marshall, that was insensitive of me. Leon? said Adam.

I'm sorry, said Leon, really, I am. But it wasn't about the sex.

Everyone looked at him or away. She was sad. I held her. It happened. Fuck me, said Adam, rolling his eyes as if he was trying to see the back of his head. Leave it, said Lauren.

Or did you go, said Evan, and all this Abbie-nurse-story-crap was just a cover-up for five thousand miles of lesbian fucking? Evan, please, said Marshall. No, he said, you can't do that, you can't make up some big elaborate story then tell us it was all a lie!

Did *you* know? asked Adam. Megan nodded. Fuck me, he said. Who else?

You told that story, didn't you, said Hannah, who'd been silent all this time, because you wanted to get it off your chest? The woman having an affair, the man jumping out of the building. She was talking to Lauren. Let it go, honey, said Leon. For fuck's sake, it just *happened*, said Lauren. I had the operation, I was feeling low, things weren't good between me and Adam. It *just happened*.

Marshall, are you okay? asked Megan. He was looking at the stairs.

Now Adam was up, out of his chair, pushing up his sleeves. You fuckhead, he said. Leon didn't respond. You fucked my wife, right after she had her breast removed. How fucked up is that? Sit down, Adam, please, said Lauren. Adam, please, said Megan. Come on mate, said Evan. Hit me, come on, said Leon. He stood up too. Don't be stupid! said Megan. Oh, don't guys, please, said Marshall. Adam lowered his fists. You're children, said Lauren. They both sat down. There was a lull.

I mean, said Evan, picking up his thread again, there you all were giving it to me about the footy scores and Megan's just told us her whole fuckin' story was a lie! Shut up Evan, said Megan. Yeah shut up Evan, said Adam.

Adam stood up again. No, he said, I'm sorry, this is completely off the scale. You can't just fuckin' say that, Lauren, in front of everybody, then sit there all smug and go like oh it *just happened*. Forget it, said Leon. No, fuck you Lee, he said; up, up, up you get, get up, get up, now! Marshall tried to hold Adam's arm but Adam threw him off. Up! he said. Leon stood. No! said Hannah. She was up too, clutching Leon to her. Adam threw his fist; it was too late to stop it. Hannah went down and Adam came down after. Fuck! screamed

Megan. Leon started thumping his own fists into the back of Adam's head. Spit was flying out of his mouth. His bald head was all blotchy and red. Evan had to drag him off and fell back onto the couch with him. Please! said Lauren.

Adam got to his feet, staggered, threw the sliding door back and walked out. The clouds had cleared, the moon was out. A herd of pigs ran down the hill to the edge of the cliff and threw themselves into the sea.

Evan held Leon in a bear hug while Leon shook and cried. Hannah was still on the floor. Leon pushed himself free, went to her and held her close. Her skirt had ridden up, there was a sliver of black satin showing. Leon was crouched right over now, as if afraid she would escape. He looked like a sad man praying.

Evan looked around. Adam was at the rail, gazing out. Lauren was on the couch: upright, jaw locked, lips tight.

Tilly was at the top of the stairs.

The commotion had brought her up. She was on the third step down, all but her head and shoulders hidden by the timber balustrade. For a moment she caught Evan's eye. She looked around: the bottles, the glasses, the tipped-over table, the tilted painting, the fire-alarm flap like a broken limb. She recorded the scene for memory and went back down again.

Evan turned to Marshall who was staring into the fire. Marshall looked at him, brought the bottle to his lips, and drank. The world's got problems, he said, it's true. But if we really put our minds to it, Evan, I reckon we can solve them.

SUNDAY

Adam was last to wake. His head was sore, his hand throbbed. A truck or tractor or something was revving somewhere on the hill. He put on some clothes and went to the kitchen where Lauren was making the coffee: she touched him on the arm.

Evan came in with an empty bowl and put it in the sink. They've been clearing the road since seven, he said, and he went out again.

Adam poured a coffee and took it out to the living room. The curtains were open, the sky had cleared, it was a cold sunny day. Megan and Marshall were at the dining table, talking, their faces close, almost touching. Marshall was holding his head. Megan was whispering, it's all right, it's all right. For some reason he was dressed in a suit. The fire door was open; Adam threw a log in and gave it a poke, then he slid the balcony door back.

The air was rich with the smell of rain. The rosellas were chattering in the trees. Leon was standing at the balcony rail, the stick in his hand, his jacket turned up to his ears. The bulldozer was loud out here, working the road below, chugging, revving. Adam stood at the rail. There was about a metre between them. Evan was below, hosing the mud off Marshall's car. It was parked across the end of the driveway now, pointing downhill, ready to go.

I'm sorry, said Leon.

Me too, said Adam.

They went quiet again.

Look at us, Ad, said Leon, without looking at him: a bunch of well-off, well-educated fucks, the generation in charge, and yet we don't know shit. We went to uni, and it didn't cost us a cent. We found jobs, made careers. Marshall's a member of parliament. We've lived off the fat. We saw the world, conquered every corner of it, but what did we ever do but stare at ourselves? We accuse that generation down there, Tilly, of being narcissistic. Yeah, well. Ours was the golden age, Ad, money to burn. We could have done something, left a legacy. But what did we do? Talked crap, argued, bickered, ate, drank—we're always eating and drinking, stuffing our faces, telling everyone what we had for breakfast, lunch and dinner. It's obscene. We've let the world go to the dogs, Adam. We've got no rigour. What did we do? I'll tell you what: we lapped at the plate they left for us until we lapped it clean.

Leon turned to look at him but Adam wasn't listening. He was looking back through the glass doors to the living room where Megan was helping Marshall out of his chair. Marshall straightened up and shook himself and gently pushed Megan away. He started walking towards the stairs. He looked terrible.

Leon looked in briefly, then turned back to the view. Okay, he said, so this is what's going on. Tilly wasn't on her phone talking to her friends. She's been at it since Friday night, right here under our noses, taking her father down. She's a troll, a good troll, mind you, working away in the dark. Facebook, Twitter, a trail of comments on every blog of every politician and journalist and commentator in the country. Marshall did this, Marshall did that, he took bribes, made false statements, rorted his travel account, embezzled party funds, bought women, went with men, took photos of himself. It's all over the net. He's a dead man walking.

But are they true? asked Adam. What? said Leon. The rumours: are they true? Leon laughed. True? Jesus, Adam, you of all people.

A wisp of white cloud was hurrying away out over the water, the sky was the deepest blue. Adam slid the door back and went inside. Leon watched him go. Down below, Evan turned off the hose, wound it back on its reel and shook his hands dry.

Tilly appeared, carrying her bag. Hannah followed, a bruise over one eye. They walked to the car. Tilly threw her bag in the back seat and got in after. Hannah closed the door. From where Leon was standing he could just see the back of Tilly's head. She was sitting up straight, her neck oddly elongated, like a princess waiting in the carriage before it sets off for the castle.

A van with a satellite dish came into view. Leon watched as it moved around the bend from behind the trees up the slope. You could see the marks the tyres made, dragging the mud up from below. A guy in a suit got out and crossed to Marshall's car. He was lifting his feet high, careful not to soil his shoes, while the driver and another guy started unloading the gear.

Now Marshall appeared, and walked down the driveway to meet them. He looked calm. He straightened his tie and extended a hand to the reporter who, confused at first, shook it. They both stood talking in the driveway, the reporter occasionally pointing to his van, then at the sky. Marshall pointed to his car, then back behind him to the house. The two guys with the gear stood at a respectful distance. The reporter gave the signal. The cameraman and boom operator set up. The light went on and Marshall blinked. The cameraman pointed with a flat hand, adjusting Marshall's position. The reporter waited, straightening the lapels of his suit.

Leon watched.

He'd been up since early morning, the only one without a hangover, to go for a run down the beach. The air had oxygen and electricity in it. He felt solid, clear, alive. The weekend faded behind. The cooking, the drinking, the talking, telling stories, the confessions, the flare-up, the look on Lauren's face, all that faded until the only thing left was the picture of Marshall in the driveway, lit by that harsh TV light, and the reporter plying him with questions.

Be careful, Marshall, thought Leon, be careful how you go. Keep it at the front of your mind, friend, that solid little nugget. *I am an honest man. A simple man. I am honest and simple and you will not undo me.* But no. Marshall was getting too animated, Leon could see him, pointing here and there, cutting the palm of one hand with the edge of the other, shaking his head too vigorously when he said no. He couldn't keep that solid nugget at the front of his mind, or—and Leon didn't want to think this—there was no nugget to keep. He kept pointing and waving and chopping and shrugging, feeding that hungry beast with every good piece of himself he had left. He was disintegrating. Even a false truth can hold up the sky, thought Leon, so long as it is solid and still. Still, Marshall, still.

The others were watching from the edge of the carport: Megan, Evan, Lauren, Adam, Hannah. They shouldn't be out there, thought Leon, they were only making things worse. He tried to get their attention, wave them back. Marshall's floundering, he wanted to say, can't you see?

He saw Megan hold her face in her hands and turn to go

inside. He saw Hannah follow. He saw Evan look up. He saw Lauren take Adam's hand. Then, strangeness upon strangeness, another noise, above the talking, coming from somewhere way out over on the other side of the hill. Marshall glanced up. The reporter and crew looked up too.

It was the TV chopper. The sound got louder. Megan came back outside and threw her arms out as if to say: What the hell? Now Marshall was throwing his arms out too. He pointed, threw a finger at the reporter, then pointed up again. The reporter clamped his hand to his ear like he was talking to his colleagues up there and maybe even asking them to back off. But the chopper kept thumping above the house. Marshall went berserk. He lunged at the reporter and tried to throw a punch; the reporter fell backwards, the boom operator stepped over him and held a straight arm out. Marshall, he was fighting. The cameraman kept shooting. Marshall hit the boom operator's hand away and lunged towards the car, screaming at Tilly inside. The cameraman was getting it all. Megan came running down the driveway and grabbed Marshall, pleading with him to stop. The others looked on. Marshall backed away. The reporter was getting to his feet, Megan was calming Marshall down but Marshall was flicking his arms left and right like the drunk in the streetfight who's been dragged.

Then everything changed again.

From below the hill, behind the trees, came a blue light,

languidly flashing. A cop car stopped below the drive. Two plain-clothes cops got out, one from each side. The first cop waved the TV reporter away and started talking to Marshall. The other cop opened the Mercedes door and asked Tilly to step outside. The reporter said something to the chopper and went back to his crew. The second cop put a hand on Tilly's back. Marshall flapped his arms. Megan moved back and forth between them. Tilly's cop led her to the car. The TV crew followed. Marshall's cop gestured to Marshall's car, indicating he should get in and follow. Marshall brushed down his suit, had some last words, flicked his hand a couple more times here and there.

Megan yelled at the reporter and pointed up at the chopper. The reporter lifted his thumb and called his crew back. Marshall got into his car. The cop car did a three-point turn and headed off down the hill. Marshall followed. The TV van followed him. Megan joined the others watching from the drive. The blue light flashed as it rounded the bend and kept flashing all the way past the muddy scar of the landslip and on down the hill.

The chopper wheeled and rose. The sea was flat and blue. They were all just specks now, way down there in the distance, winding along the Great Ocean Road. The cameraman was checking his footage, the reporter writing his lead. The boom operator, tired from driving (he'd been up since five), was watching Marshall's brake lights brighten and dull. There was a swoop and swoosh as they rounded the bends. Marshall was watching the back of Tilly's head, her black hair hanging down. Tilly, for her part, was thumbing her phone. The cop checked the mirror. Turn it off now, please, he said.